NATE:

A Father and Son Story

by Stuart Suskind

All Rights Reserved. No part of this publication may be reproduced in any form or by any means, including scanning, photocopying, or otherwise without prior written permission of the copyright holder except in the case of brief quotations embodied in critical articles and reviews.

Copyright Stuart Suskind © 2018

ISBN 13: 978-1-944662-28-8

This is a work of fiction. Names, characters, places and incidents are the product of the author's imagination or are used fictitiously. Any resemblance to actual events, locals, or persons, living or dead, is entirely coincidental.

Cover Design by MASGraphicarts.com © 2018

Dedication

This book is lovingly dedicated to my wife Cherry in appreciation for her unending encouragement and support.

Contents

NATE: i

A Father and Son Story i

Dedication iii

Acknowledgments vi

About the Author vii

PREFACE ix

Chapter 1 1

Chapter 2 14

Chapter 3 17

Chapter 4 22

Chapter 5 30

Chapter 6 34

Chapter 7 46

Chapter 8 58

Chapter 9 63

Chapter 10	75
Chapter 11	81
Chapter 12	88
Chapter 13	91
Chapter 14	94
Chapter 15	105
Chapter 16	110
Chapter 17	115
Chapter 18	117
Chapter 19	121
Chapter 20	124
Chapter 21	127
Chapter 22	133
Chapter 23	138
Chapter 24	142
Chapter 25	148
Chapter 26	153

Chapter 27 159

Chapter 28 165

Chapter 29 173

Chapter 30 181

Chapter 31 184

Chapter 32 191

Acknowledgments

My thanks to my sisters Phyllis Josell and Ruth Ann Burk who share many rich memories of Nate and to my wonderful daughters, Jill Suskind, high school English teacher, and Judy Bell, nurse and mother. I would also express my gratitude to Dr. Albert M. Bromberg of Somers, New York (who inspired Dr. Abrahams), to Rev. Newsom Holmes and to Rabbi Yisroel Cotlar for their thoughts and insights.

About the Author

Stuart on left with his father

Stuart Suskind holds advanced degrees in chemistry and law and has worked in related fields over his entire career. He first was employed for product development and later as a patent practitioner in pharmaceuticals.

Although modified by his teen years in Binghamton New York, he still has a tinge of a Brooklyn accent and still enjoys visiting his old Bensonhurst neighborhood.

He has continued playing the clarinet in community bands and is still in search of the perfect tennis forehand.

He currently lives in Cary, North Carolina with his wife and can be reached at stuartsuskind@att.net.

He has been a technical ghostwriter for several South American universities writing patent and market research reports in the fields of pharmaceuticals, biology and agricultural chemistry.

PREFACE

I had always said that I would not cry at his funeral. There I stood, frozen, looking down on him wrapped in a traditional prayer shawl and white satin skull cap reminding me of past High Holy Days as we proudly stood together in worship—father and son.

He had died for me many years earlier, maybe around 13 or 14. That doesn't mean that I had stopped loving him.

Mine was a love and admiration that I have never seen among children. None of my friends broke away from our street games to run and meet their father walking home from the subway. I would grab his arm and walk home with him and then probably sit with him on the couch as he read the evening paper. What's more, I knew of no other kid who at the age of five or six understood the rules of the game of baseball as I did. Yes, many of my friends knew the teams and the scores, but they couldn't explain some of the complicated plays like I could. I knew the game very well, but why not? We sat together listening to the Dodger games on the radio with the noisy crowds in the background or with the quiet clicking of the teletype. We listened as Red Barber gave the play-by-play, and we talked about the game just as if we were two old friends sitting at a bar. And if that doesn't convince you, how many kids had a father who could keep them laughing almost constantly. Of course, a lot of his stuff was silly, but he had a presentation and a style that made his jokes, often one-liners, very funny. At six feet tall with an athletic build combined with a natural smile and his warmth and acceptance of everybody, he was like a movie star to me; incredibly, he saw humor in almost everything.

When I say he died for me, I mean that his passing was a slow process occurring subconsciously. His death for me was a gradual realization of his limitations and their profound effect on those around him.

As I stood there staring at him, many childhood scenes passed through my mind with a mixture of feelings some happy, some sad. A strange heaviness came over me as I pondered the question of how a boy could lose his attachment to the father he had loved so much. Suddenly my knees weakened. I quickly covered my face with my handkerchief and finally broke down.

Chapter 1

There was a soul up in heaven waiting its turn to be matched with a human being at birth. This soul was independent, impatient and very cynical about the state of the world and the people who inhabited it. When the Lord was ready to unite the soul with a new human being, the soul complained to the Lord:

"Please, please don't do this to me. The world is such an unhappy place; there is so much fighting and struggling and unhappiness. I don't want to be part of it."

The Lord took pity on this poor soul and contemplated, out of love, how the problem might be resolved. Finally, the Lord presented the idea of uniting the soul with a human being destined to become a man of great humor, a man who would keep the soul entertained, laughing and in good spirits.

Nate

Nate Rubin started his business career as a window dresser for a New York City haberdashery. His ability to freehand sketch along with a good eye for colors and design gave him a knack for eye-catching window displays and interesting arrangements of merchandise inside the store. He could take a stock of uninteresting hats and give them eye appeal. Not that hats were unimportant at that point in fashion history. No self-respecting person would be seen in public without a hat. Hats were an essential element of dress. For men, the matching of suit and hat made a key statement of personality. Hats had a role in everyday social contacts. For example, a hat might be lifted or tipped down to greet or acknowledge another person. Men knew or were supposed to know when it was proper to remove their hats. In all the new Hollywood talking movies, detectives and FBI agents wore hats, which miraculously stayed in place during fast, exciting chase scenes.

Hats of all sizes, shapes, and colors paraded down 5th Avenue on Easter Sunday and were photographed for the universe to see and admire.

Before the end of the century, though, hats would lose their place in the average wardrobe, and the hat industry would dwindle in size; no one anticipated this, so "keep it under your hat!"

Nate pleased his store manager and was well liked by the entire staff partly through his decorating skills and partly for his warm personality and spontaneous mood-lifting humor.

He was optimistic and felt confident in his future. Even without a college degree his natural abilities would bring him success in the business world. His parents and sisters did not share that confidence and encouraged him to continue his education. Nate knew that as a student he had never seriously studied. His dislike for school and studies ran so deep that he turned down athletic scholarships in track, baseball, and football to the University of Michigan, his high school coach's alma mater.

Bachelor life in New York City in the 1920s was sweet for Nate. He made a decent living and presented himself as an attractive, appealing young man. At six feet tall with a trim athletic build and a warm and engaging personality, he easily made female friends. To his great enjoyment, he had the Brooklyn Dodgers and New York Yankees baseball on the radio in the summer and professional football in the fall. He loved the brilliant entertainment of the New York stage and vaudeville. His favorite comedians, including Groucho Marx, George Burns, Jack Benny, Milton Berle, and many others, became models of style and presentation of humor. Nate watched and learned the art of being funny—the voice, timing, body language—leading eventually to his own style of humor. In his 20s he became a laughable, likeable comedian.

The haberdashery business was growing, and his employer added new stores along the East Coast and as far west as Louisville, Kentucky. Nate was asked to travel to these new stores to help set up displays in store windows. Occasionally he was asked to help with a difficult customer. He could entertain a woman while she tried on hats and rarely left the store empty-handed. Recognizing this talent, his manager offered him a position in sales.

At age 32 Nate was given the opportunity to manage a new store opening in Binghamton, New York.

"Of all my wife's relations, I like myself the best."
—Nate Rubin

Based on everything that I have ever heard about her and upon some of the pictures and snapshots that we had in the house, my mother was a beautiful young lady—smart, warm-hearted, well-liked, and a pretty good pianist.

I suppose she would have been justified in thinking that she would marry a terrific guy, have some great children, and live a wonderful life. Unfortunately, she would be denied.

Her first husband, my sister's father, impressed her family as a man she deserved. He was handsome, outgoing, and appeared to be in love. His interest in gambling and drinking seemed to be merely his way of having some fun; however, after a few years, it was no longer under control and a great concern to everybody. He would disappear for days. She could not stick to a budget because money would be mysteriously spent. She was sadly disappointed when the money they put away for a piano or for a new winter coat disappeared—gambled away. Eventually it was clear that he had a serious gambling and drinking problem, and she lost all hope in the future of their marriage.

Dora decided to leave him and get a divorce. A difficult choice with a three-year-old child at a time when divorces were not common. Her earning power was limited. Separated from her husband, with a three-year-old child, she turned to her family for support. Fortunately, her parents had plenty of room in their house, and two married sisters lived close by. Although the economy was weak and jobs not plentiful, she found a position as a saleslady in a women's hat store, where she worked with several other attractive, friendly young ladies under a dashing (she thought), good-looking manager who was none other than Nate Rubin, her future husband.

She was a welcome addition to his staff as the customers liked her, and he was attracted to her good looks and her warm, open way of relating to people. While he was surrounded by many pretty women, she was special. Chemistry was working, and he wasted no time in asking her out to dinner.

Sitting across from him, she stared, smiled, and laughed, feeling a much-needed therapy given the sadness that had settled into her life. She was a welcome audience to his jokes, stories, and silly antics. There was a kind of camaraderie between them, not surprising since both their parents had come to America from nearby towns in eastern Poland only about 30 years earlier.

As their relationship grew, she invited him home where he enjoyed the tasty food and warm open welcome from her parents and her sisters. They laughed and told stories and ate ethnic foods together. He enjoyed his time with her family which was certainly an improvement over being home alone at his bachelor pad. The women he had been seeing, while charming and good-looking, fell short in this cultural area which held deep feelings for many Jews.

He, in turn, reminded her parents of their days back in the *shtetl i*n Poland and of a traveling entertainer by the name of Moshe Spivak.

"Yes, I remember at the close of the Sabbath, how we women would rush to the kitchen in the back hall of the synagogue where we began preparing some dishes and talking about who might be coming to entertain us that evening," Dora's mother said.

"Yes, and Mordecai would leave his violin in the hall, and Solomon his clarinet. Before you knew it, we were having some warm soup and listening to such bright wonderful music," my grandfather added.

They were carried back to some of their best memories of what was a hard life back in Poland.

"Our best times were on those evenings when it was our turn to have Moshe back, to sit with us, make us laugh, and talk to us. At that time many of us were worrying that the warm welcome the king had offered the Jews back in the 16th century to come live in Poland might be wearing off. Well, it makes sense. The king brought us there to improve the economy and the level of education, but some of the Polish people, bearing some anti-Semitism of the time, were not so happy."

Spivak also had a way of stimulating discussions about some issues that were connected to religion, social behavior, and issues of the time. For example, the concept of the righteous man always brought around some lively discussion. Some would argue that a righteous man, a *tzadik,* cared about social justice while for others he was a man of great moral principle. Some people expressed a new thought that the righteous man was a person who actively sought and found ways to help the weak, sick, and the poor.

"Let me tell you a funny story about a righteous man," Spivak offered the gathering. Speaking in Yiddish, he told this story that my grandparents later told my mother and her siblings—also in Yiddish—and which she translated into English for my family and friends one evening. Her translation lost none of the hilarious quality of this story.

"I want to tell you about Yaakov, a religious Jew who always tried to do the right thing, always thought of himself or at least hoped to be considered a righteous man.

"Well, it seems that Yaakov came home from the synagogue one Friday night with a black eye."

"Yaakov, how did you get such a black eye?" his wife inquired.

"Well, it all started last week at Sabbath service," he answered. "I was sitting quietly alone praying and who should come in but that fat lady Goldberg— you know the one with the big tuches—and sits down right in front of me. Comes time to stand up, her dress gets caught between her legs in her crotch (turning and showing the hidden region)…"

"I know where you're talking about; you don't have to show me. So, what happened next?"

"I reached in and pulled it out. She quickly took her purse, turned around, and gave me a shot right in the head."

"Okay, so how did you get a black eye tonight?"

"Tonight, I'm sitting next to my good friend Jacob, and we are praying together. In comes the same fat lady Goldberg, and again she sits right in front of me. Again, comes time to stand up, her dress is again getting caught—same place. This time my friend reaches and pulls it out, but I remember from last week that she doesn't like that, so I pushed it back in (thrusting his right arm forward)."

This story never failed to evoke laughter in the group.

My grandparents had a great fondness for Nate and had an enjoyable time with him. He in turn felt at home and enjoyed entertaining them. Along with the attraction that my mother and Nate had for each other, this environment brought them closer, much closer.

"How many months are you?" he inquired gently.

"It's almost two months now. I know my body very well and I'm sure that I'm pregnant. In fact, I know the exact night it happened."

He took a few deep breaths and quietly began to ponder his entire life situation. He was 31 years old, free and independent. There were plenty of good-looking women around and some good ballgames on the radio. He liked to listen to the comedians like Jack Benny and the detective programs like *Gangbusters*. So, life was good and uncomplicated, and he had very little interest in marriage and in raising a family. He had never thought about earning enough money to support a wife and children.

"We might consider an abortion; after all, you are still married."

"But it's illegal and so expensive, and I couldn't face my family."

"From everything I've heard and read, in 1935 abortions are carried out all the time. Family doctors like your Dr. Morrison can recommend skilled and experienced doctors who can perform the procedure under clean, safe conditions and then follow-up later for a good recovery. The state of New York like many other states is mainly concerned with safety and cleanliness."

"But, Nate, it will take thousands of dollars, and I have no idea where we can get that much money. All of my family and friends believe that we love each other and that we should welcome the offspring of our love."

"If we are going to marry, we should start thinking now about a divorce; and for sure your parents and my parents will insist on a divorce in the Jewish religion."

"You mean a ghet."

"Yes, and we will have to get your taxi-driving husband to appear with us in the Rabbi's office."

Nate started to take all the necessary steps. He was motivated by the idea of doing the right thing for Dora by giving her marriage and family for her pretty little girl, who he liked very much. He would be proud to say to all, especially to Dora's family, that this was the right thing to do, and no joking about it. Deep down, though, he had doubts about all this new responsibility and about earning enough money to support a family. He ignored his doubts and fears and went into action.

He took the subway downtown to one of the busy taxicab stands where he asked the whereabouts of Dora's husband and finally found him at a luncheon counter.

"So, you're the guy who has been dating Dora. I have tried many times to get us back together. I believe we love each other. I have my faults, but I have always loved her. I regret that I have done some very hurtful things to her."

"We are planning to marry and have come to ask you to help us get a divorce and to come to the Rabbi's office to get a ghet."

"And are you so sure that you will be a better husband and that she loves you?"

"Well, I may never do her much good, but for sure I will never do her any harm."

Nate and Dora were married in her parents' home, and I was born the following September weighing in at a hefty nine plus pounds. Until our teens, my sister and I had no idea that Nate was not her natural father.

My grandparents saw Nate as a blessing and for

good reason. He appeared to be a stay-at-home guy and a lot of fun to be around. He also seemed to be willing to take care of Dora and her daughter.

Soon after my birth, Nate changed careers by taking a position in Brooklyn as an agent with Prudential Insurance.

Chapter 2

It was the summer of my eighth birthday. The plan was for me to spend a couple of weeks with my grandparents at their cottage in the Catskills. Mother and I traveled to the Greyhound station in New York City, where I would join my Aunt Ruth for a three-hour trip up state.

I had a tremendous admiration for my Aunt Ruth. She had raised two sons about seven or eight years older than me in an apartment in the Bronx where they shared a bedroom and an elaborate chemistry set and where I witnessed the most amazing experiments and tricks. The array of chemicals, flames, and glassware transported me to another world while in their bedroom. My uncle was a rabbi with a dignified look and style who played classical music on the radio. To my surprise he had a playful side which I first noticed as he teased my sister and pinched her butt, all with a big, friendly smile.

I hugged and kissed my aunt as we boarded the bus. Once in our seats she presented me with a toy soldier attached to a small cloth parachute. She would share the fun in the field next to the cottage throwing it up in the air and watching it drift down. This was an exciting thought for a boy who, like others my age, followed war stories about the Army and Air Force and the Navy fighting against the Germans and the Japanese.

I took the window seat with her next to me, then looked out the window and saw my mother standing alone with a look of sadness and loneliness on her face, an expression I knew well and would never forget. My mood changed immediately. I believe the sadness in her eyes was something only I was aware of. After all, she was a good-looking woman, joyful and warm, with the unique ability to listen to others with 110% attention. I believe that most people were so engaged in the love and warmth of her personality and her giving they missed that hint of melancholy in her eyes.

The bus driver raced the engines, then closed the door. In panic I forced myself to the aisle and ran to the exit, yelling, "Open the door!" I jumped down the steps and ran over to my mother.

I don't remember which thought dominated me—either she can't get along without me or I can't get along without her. I do remember, though, how frightened I was.

We went home together, and I was happy to be back home in my neighborhood even though I knew I would be teased about being shamefully tied to my mother's apron strings.

Here was a strange paradox: I had this beautiful, caring mother that I loved and a father that I was so attached to. I felt so lucky thinking that no other kid had a set of parents like mine. Yet, somehow, I was deeply troubled knowing that none of my friends would have been so compelled to run back to their mother giving up that trip to the Catskills. That thought was unsettling, and I pushed it out of my mind.

Years later I would connect the sadness in her eyes to my panic on the bus and finally to my gradual loss of a father.

Chapter 3

With a wide smile, I listened to stories of my father's boyhood and especially enjoyed hearing about his athletic prowess in baseball, football, and track, although I could not picture him as an athlete. After all, I had never seen him participate in anything athletic. I saw him walk home from the subway, and I saw him on the couch reading the newspaper and not much else. He did show me a medal that he had won at track meet, and this was, with only one exception, the only tangible evidence of his athletic youth. We were walking to the subway train station one day when we heard the roar of the approaching train.

"We might miss it," he said. "Let's run." His legs moved fast and his long stride was something that I noticed only years later at a track meet, realizing that indeed Nate had been a track star.

Nate

I was proud of the idea of my father as an athlete but to visualize it I had to rely mainly on my fantasy. It was confusing. Why did he so completely give up all athletic activity? Maybe it wasn't true—all just a nice story.

Future events would shed some light on this mysterious contradiction. One of these would come in a most unexpected way.

One summer we vacationed in the Catskills at a hotel that had no restaurant—if you can call this a vacation—but instead all families had a small gas burner and a section of a refrigerator. The mothers stood in somewhat cramped quarters cooking meals for their families on the small gas stove, having an enjoyable time talking loudly to each other in mixtures of English and Yiddish. The dining room was large and dark with many tables. The air carried the smell of linseed oil from the oil cloth table covers. Flypaper covered with trapped flies hung from the ceiling. Dinner time was hot, smelly, and noisy. I had very little appetite. Upstairs there was one bathroom for the entire floor—another turn-off. I went hungry and constipated most of the time, which, of course, made my mother unhappy.

The bright spot came on weekends when the fathers, after working all week in the city, came up to join us. I was overjoyed at that idea until on one Sunday morning at breakfast we were all invited on the loudspeaker to come to the softball field, where all the men were going to play ball. All the men I had known in my admittedly short life seemed more aggressive, forceful, and self-confident than my father, who, while very funny, was mainly a newspaper reader, so I had some anxieties about him competing against the other fathers. My image of myself compared to others my age was somewhat similar. I immediately pictured my father as clumsy or inept at catching or hitting a softball. Somewhat reluctantly I sat down on the ground near third base and waited sadly for his humiliation in front of all the other fathers.

Those who know some baseball history may be familiar with the story of how on one occasion Babe Ruth stepped up to the plate, turned to his loyal fans in the stands, and pointed to the outfield bleachers in a way that suggested to all that he was going to clobber one up there into the stands. He did not disappoint his many followers.

Nate stepped up to the home plate for his first at bat, and, in Babe Ruth style, looked over to me sitting on the ground near third base and pointed toward far off left field. Before I had a chance to absorb what he meant, on the next pitch, he swung the bat hitting the ball with a loud crack, practically knocking its cover off, sending the ball high and deep into left field.

The next look back into his youth came later that summer. At age nine or 10, I confronted the fact that in athletics I rated low among my peers as evidenced by being one of the last picked for a team whether in a street game or school recess. These moments of truth were hurtful and left a lasting impression. While I was a good student and even a leader in school and very well-liked by my friends, this low rating of my athletic skills was a tremendous blow to my ego. Somewhere at a lower level of conscious, well-hidden, was the gnawing question of why my father and I were at opposite ends of the athletic spectrum and why in heaven's name he had totally neglected helping me in anything resembling athletics.

One summer day I took my damaged ego to my mother and cried that I could not play ball as well as my friends. I could not catch or throw the ball.

"Why are you coming to me," she said. "I can't help you. You should go to your father."

I did not know the answer to that question except that she always seemed to know the solution to my troubles.

He did come outside with me and showed me the proper way to throw a ball. We stood on the curb on opposite sides of the street, throwing back and forth. Things were going along smoothly when

I noticed that his grip on the ball was changing and looking rather odd. The next ball he threw came straight at me, but, about two feet before it reached my hands, it dropped just as if it had rolled off a table. The next balls he threw swerved to the side or dropped down to the ground. It was like a magic act. I could hardly catch the ball—partly because it moved around so and partly because I was laughing so hard I could hardly stand up.

And so now my fantasies of Nate as a young man were filled in by his mighty swing at the bat and his lively, unpredictable deliveries from the pitcher's mound. The man I loved and admired for his jokes and fun was indeed an athlete. He could hit and pitch and that was amazing. Okay, for some odd reason, he had become inactive, but nevertheless he had been a great athlete.

Chapter 4

I grew up in what was essentially a self-contained universe. The houses in my Brooklyn neighborhood were comprised of two attached four-family brick structures each with a set of stairs leading to the front door with a slab of concrete between each set. This area, known as the "stoop," was the center of social activity as people sat on the stairs or on the slab to converse, play cards, and just hang out.

There were about 15 of these eight-family units on my street or "block" as they were often called. The corners were busy commercial areas. To the right facing south toward Coney Island was a drugstore, a vegetable market, a candy store, a Chinese laundry, and a small grocery store. On the left corner was another grocery store, a small bagel factory, a shoe repair shop, a barbershop, and a small Orthodox synagogue.

Nate

Two movie theaters were a 10-minute walk away located on one of the busiest, longest avenues in Brooklyn. On most Saturday afternoons, we would watch moving pictures of the war, cops and robbers, or cowboys. The price of the ticket for kids was $.11, which we scraped together by returning glass "deposit" bottles. Milk, cream, and soda were purchased in glass bottles that, after rinsing, could be redeemed at the store for the two or five-cent deposits. My friends and I would start our trip to the movie with armfuls of glass deposit bottles.

Our local theaters introduced air-conditioning in the middle of a very hot summer. People went to the movies just get some relief from the heat. We shared ideas about what air-conditioning was all about and how it would feel, but it remained a mystery until we walked up to the ticket taker and entered the theater into the darkness and were suddenly surrounded by cold, winter-like air with the aroma of popcorn and freshly vacuumed carpeting.

There were many kids on my block all about the same age, and we became friends starting at kindergarten age. These friendships often lasted through high school. We were all proud of Brooklyn and thought of it as the second capital after D.C. Some of my friends stayed there until young adult age. My best friend lived on the opposite side of the street. As babies, we had been wheeled in carriages by our fathers on weekends. We played together in the street in our homes talking baseball like true Brooklyn Dodger fans.

The "candy stores" in Brooklyn were not exclusively for candy. They were luncheonettes, small toy stores, and places to buy school supplies, newspapers, and magazines. The candy stores had a characteristic and pleasing odor that emanated from a combination of the sweet berry smell of bubblegum along with a popular drink made at the counters called egg creams. The egg cream was eggless. It was made from a mixture of chocolate syrup, a splash of milk, and seltzer water. This mixture had a characteristic milky, chocolatey aroma. Many candy stores had a soda counter on the outside wall so in the summer people could walk by and order an egg cream without going into the store.

The bubblegum, which sold for a penny, apparently was processed on machines that put teeth-like indentations into the gum. On one occasion my mother gave me a penny to get myself a piece of bubble gum. When I arrived home, she decided that the indentations were human and that someone had bitten into that piece of gum. She made an appearance at the candy store and argued with the female proprietor who was always at the soda counter facing the very large mirror the line the opposing wall. I thought this woman was quite strange, because she would talk to her customers by looking at them in the mirror. This reminded me of my dentist who always looked at my teeth through a mirror instead of directly at them.

In front of the store, a large wooden newsstand held the New York papers including the New York Daily News, The Mirror, the Herald Tribune, The Post and the New York Times. Because the Sunday Times was so thick, extra stands were added to handle the piles of Sunday Times. It kept Nate busy reading and listening to the ball game for the rest of the day on Sundays.

Nate was a steady Sunday Times customer. I would walk with him Sunday morning after breakfast to pick up his copy. In the nice weather, people were outside hanging around their stoop. Nate's friends would stand near the curb talking about the war and smoking cigars. On our way home, we would join them. Nate gave his opinion about the progress of the war and spoke with great authority, probably because he read more than anyone else. He liked to show me off because the men had discovered that I could add a column of numbers in my head. They would challenge me with a list of five or six numbers and were amazed, it seemed, when I gave them the answer. It was fun for me, and I was happy to make my father proud.

Summer weekend evenings brought the card games on my block. The men would carry chairs and a bridge table out to the sidewalk and drape a lightbulb over a tree branch wired back through an open window. They quietly played poker, pinochle, or gin rummy and lost their money till the wee hours under a heavy cloud of smoke which kept the mosquitoes as well as me and my friends away.

1947 was an exciting year for 12-year-olds like me and my friends in our Brooklyn neighborhood. The Brooklyn Dodgers won the National League pennant and would face the New York Yankees in the World Series. To add to the excitement, this was the first year the series would be televised. We let our imaginations run wild as we had never seen a TV and had no hope of watching the World Series on television, because none of us had one. We spent many hours fantasizing about how the Dodgers would look hitting and fielding and pitching in our living room. We had images of Pee-wee Reese scooping up a ground ball, starting a double play at second base—all in our living room.

We were not a mean or bullying bunch of guys, but we had certain standards of behavior and there was a unique chemistry among us. In our neighborhood, though, there were a few kids we rejected possibly because they were wimpy or cried a lot. We tried to get along with them, but it just didn't work, and we often found ourselves chasing them home crying to their mothers. Howie was one of these kids, and it was Howie who taught us how fate can twist things around even among young schoolboys.

About two weeks before the series began, Howie appeared before us announcing proudly that his parents were purchasing a television and that he, emboldened with newfound power, would be selectively inviting his friends to come in and watch the World Series. Of course, we did not qualify as friends and we knew it. However, we had enough street smarts to manipulate Howie into believing that we were his friends or at least would become friends in the future. In time we were able to wrangle an invitation from him to watch the first game on TV in his living room.

On the day of the game, we all lined up in front of his house, walking past his mother as she held the front door open. She was a loving and kind lady. She looked at us all carefully as we filed by and in somewhat of a naïve, innocent expression said, "I didn't know Howie had so many friends."

During the following years, we all grew up and matured a little; Howie became one of our best friends. We spent many long hours together watching baseball on TV.

Chapter 5

My sister, who was five years older, and I played the same games in the streets and sidewalks and loved the same cartoon characters. At home she played with dolls and girls' toys which she often shared with me but under strict control.

On Sunday mornings, we got up early before my parents and shared the *Sunday New York News* color comics. There was lox and bagels on the table that my parents had purchased the night before. I sliced my bagel with a butter knife, the only knife I could use and mangled it badly. I imitated my sister's technique for putting cream cheese on the bagel and pressing out small pieces of the lox with a fork.

We listened to children's programs on the radio and sang along as proud New Yorkers:

Eastside, Westside all around the town.

The tots play 'ring 'round Rosie,'

'London Bridges falling down.'

Boys and girls together,

Me and Mamie O'Rourke,

We tripped the light fantastic

On the sidewalks of New York

℘ ℘

Beyond the actual necessities, my parents spent very little money on me or my sister. They just didn't have much to spend on us. We did get by, though, with nice clothes on the high holidays and all the school equipment we needed.

My sister complained during our teenage years that I was treated much better than she. Hearing this, I took some time to look back as far as I could remember. She was given plenty of love and attention by my parents and relatives. When it comes to gifts and toys and things kids want, we were both frequently denied. It seemed to me that we were treated equally.

There was one event, however, that may have been traumatic, an experience that may have affected her thinking.

We used to visit my grandparents in the Bronx on Sundays about every other month. We took the subway from lower Brooklyn up to the middle of the Bronx, which took about an hour. On one train ride home, about 9:00 in the evening, we arrived at our station in Brooklyn and walked out onto the platform. It was a dark November evening; there was a hint of winter in the air.

My sister was not with us. We were in shock.

"Where is she? Didn't she get off the train with us?" I felt scared. She had been reading on the way home with her head buried in a book as she often did and didn't see us get off the train. Nate sized up the situation thinking out loud:

"I could take the next train to the next stop but how would I know that she got off at the next stop? She might stay on for a couple more stops. And then when she gets off she might cross over and take a train back faster than I can get there. Let's wait on the other side for another train to come back. And that's what we did, but she was not on that train. My parents decided that there was no way to find her on the subway and that we should go home and wait for her. She would know her way back, and she no doubt had a nickel fare to get on a train back.

She appeared at our front door about an hour later explaining that she had asked a man on the train for help. He had walked her across to the other platform and waited for a train with her, reminding her of the correct station stop. She walked home alone from the train station.

I don't know what she was thinking during that ordeal. Did she cry? Was she scared? Did she feel abandoned or neglected? Wasn't it my parents' responsibility to make sure their 14-year-old daughter got off that train? Did she blame them? I don't know the answers, because she would never talk about it again. But I do give her credit for being so brave.

I have asked myself many times how my parents could have gotten off that train without their 14-year-old daughter.

Chapter 6

The gang of kids on my block became friends at the early age of around five or six when our mothers let us play outdoors by ourselves. We improvised games on the sidewalks using an assortment of things we found from chalk to worn shoe heels. Sydney "Buddy" Epstein, pushy and loud, emerged as a natural leader. He organized our play and kept us together like a sort of glue. Aggressive, tough talking, fist flying, and feisty, Buddy had a way of making things happen even among five to six-year-olds. He was a standout, shoes generally untied, legs and knees dirtier than most of us, always dissatisfied and looking for something more exciting to do like punching other kids. I got into many fights with him and ended up back home crying.

"Buddy Epstein hit me again," I sobbed.

"Don't play with him anymore; just stay away from him. Just walk away when you see him," my mother would respond.

In time Buddy mellowed and became slightly more socialized and less belligerent. During that period, I grew to like him mainly because he always had original ideas and new things to do or talk about. But there was always a bad boy side to him that manifested clearly a few years later.

We attended Hebrew School in the little synagogue on the corner of our block where he became impatient and annoyed by the tiny quarters of our little schoolroom and the somewhat disorganized quality of our classes with the rabbi. My sister was also enrolled, and she and the other girls would take Hebrew classes separately with the rabbi's wife in their attached apartment. While teaching she took care of her infant, and my sister complained that the whole room smelled like urine.

Buddy's dissatisfaction led to predictable misbehavior on his part, and he finally got expelled. In response, his parents apologized to the rabbi and enrolled him in a synagogue that was about six blocks away. They were accustomed to adjustments like this.

"You should see the nice classroom in my new Hebrew school—just like regular school. And the rabbi's wife is our teacher and she is so nice. Walk over there with me and I'll show you what I mean," he bragged to me.

Now I was envious of Buddy and wanted to be in that school with him, but my request was turned down by my parents. Not to be denied, I found a way to annoy the rabbi. We all sat at a long table that was old and unstable, so I sat at one end and with my knee I caused the table to rock forward gently into the rabbi who finally got exasperated with my behavior and kicked me out.

I interpreted this as being expelled, but my mother learned otherwise. She was president of the Ladies Auxiliary, and this was particularly embarrassing for her. She spoke to the rabbi and learned he was only responding to that day and wanted me back.

"No, no, I'm not going back there; he kicked me out and I know that he doesn't want me back," I exaggerated to my mother.

I finally got my way and joined Buddy. The fact that I liked it so much, was doing so well, and getting compliments on my work did, in fact, please my parents, and so the whole episode had a peaceful conclusion. The problem for the rabbi persisted though as my other friends also quit so that we could all be together. This hurt the rabbi's revenue stream, so he was forced to make some adjustments which ultimately turned out to be the best thing for him and his school.

During this whole episode, my father's response was simply to relate his Hebrew school days and how the class gave the rabbi, who spoke with a thick Eastern European accent, such a tough time. During roll call some of the kids would murmur "here" to cover for a boy who was playing hooky that day. The rabbi caught on to this antic and firmly admonished, "Let the absent ones answer for themselves," and this led to a roar of laughter.

My parents were tolerant of my friendship with Buddy, but deep down they had concerns that sooner or later it would lead to some trouble. Little did they expect that the trouble would come over something as innocuous as breakfast cereal and the comics.

The comics/cartoons were loved back then by men, women, and children of all ages. They appeared in daily newspapers and in color on weekends, in comic books, in the movies, on radio, and on bubble gum wrappers. From Dick Tracy to Donald Duck to Wonder Woman, we all had our favorites. For me it was the *Superman* broadcast 15 minutes each day on the radio after school sponsored by Kellogg's Pep, a breakfast cereal that no one liked. The Pep flakes looked innocent enough, but they soaked up milk and formed a thick sludge on the bottom of the bowl.

The Kellogg's people tried several gimmicks to encourage kids to eat that cereal. They would offer various rings and toys and books on the *Superman* radio program in exchange for mailing in $.10 and a box top from the cereal. Apparently even this was not successful, so they tried a more direct approach by putting things like Superman pictures and books and even a model airplane to be cut out of the sheet of balsam wood in the cereal box itself.

They finally came up with a winner when they created an enameled metal button found in the cereal to be pinned on clothing with a shiny and colorful picture of one of the famous comic book characters. I discussed these prize buttons with Buddy.

"I see you have a button from Kellogg's Pep; wait, wow, you've got two of them. How did you get two?"

"My mother bought me two boxes."

"Will she buy you another?"

"No, and she's mad at me because I won't eat the cereal."

Nate

"Me too. I got halfway through and can't finish."

"We tried to feed it to my dog, but he won't eat it either."

"I wanted Superman but got Popeye."

An idea entered my mind. "Do you still have that little pen knife?"

"Yeah."

"That knife could cut right through a box of cereal. At the grocery store, we could grab a button right out of the box and then run like crazy."

"Yeah, but we'd get caught; everyone would see us."

"You know that new supermarket on 18th Avenue? The cereal shelf is all the way back in the corner of the store."

We talked and talked finally convincing each other that we could cut open boxes in the back of that store and get away with at least 10 buttons.

Entering the new supermarket after school, we grabbed a shopping cart and walked up the aisle to the rear. After grabbing five or six Pep boxes, we turned and went down the next aisle. As we walked, Buddy cut open the boxes with his pen knife, and I pulled out the buttons one at a time. Then we turned and walked back up the aisle to return the boxes to their rightful place undisturbed, whereupon we were confronted by a tough-looking guy with a face badly in need of a shave.

"What the hell are you two doing? Is this what they teach you in school now?"

Then he grabbed our arms and forced us back into a storage room. He pushed us down on some boxes and then raised a large sardine can threatening to hit us over the head.

Trembling and crying, Buddy and I promised never to do it again.

"One of you is going home to get the money to pay for this cereal. Six boxes at $.11 each."

Buddy went home, and I stayed. While waiting for his return, I saw a woman standing high on a ladder peering through a hole in the wall. On the way home, I described to Buddy exactly how we got caught.

Dinner was over when I got home, so I quietly ate alone. The incident was never discussed.

Kellogg's Pep was eventually taken off the market and never appeared again in stores.

With my 12th birthday I started seventh grade in the junior high school that stood on the corner of the next block. My friends and I were all excited about the new experiences that awaited us except for one lingering doubt. We had heard that physical education would require taking showers in the nude. We had been together since first grade but had never undressed in front of each other.

We slowly, quietly entered the gym on that day of The First Shower. Undressing went slowly, deliberately, but, finally, urged on through the impatient encouragement of the teacher, we got into the shower where the warm water tended to put us a little more at ease. Eventually out of curiosity I took a good look at the other boy's genital area but found nothing of great interest as none of us had any pubic hair and our genitals looked more like a teapot spout. Charlie Miller was an exception. We noticed to our astonishment that Charlie had a much larger penis and a lot of pubic hair. Some months later when we first heard the term "hung," we said, "Oh, you mean like Charlie Miller."

Without intending to hurt Charlie or insult him, we asked, "Are you sure you're not two or three years older than the rest of us," or "Charlie, were you left back a few times?"

The shock of discovering Charlie's early maturity wore off after a few more showers and things got back to normal with Charlie who had always been a likeable friend. Looking back, I had noticed that Charlie's voice had changed a couple of years sooner than the rest of us. Hormones on a fast track!

I saw Charlie in a slightly different light and perhaps I listened more carefully to him and maybe respected him a little bit more than other boys. It's like in the song "If I Were Rich Man" from the show *Fiddler on the Roof* where Tevye sings that a rich man is given a better seat in the synagogue and people listen extra carefully to a him because they think he "really knows." To my 12-year-old mind, to be hung like Charlie meant that he is mature and probably "really knows."

For me and many of my friends, the most difficult issues and challenges of teen years dealt with manhood or masculinity. Now, if you mentioned that to a Brooklyn kid, you would have been advised with certainty that you were crazy in colorful language accompanied by all kinds of arm and finger movements. We were extremely sensitive about our masculinity. Yet we knew that issues involving physical strength, athletic ability, being liked by girls, and penis size were deeply involved in our image of who we were as young men. In fact, we heard it sung on the radio, "You gotta be a football hero to get along with the beautiful girls."

One clever advertiser for a bodybuilding company showed a little story in cartoon style which began with a good-looking, skinny boy on a beach enjoying the sun with his pretty girlfriend. Next came along a musclebound brute who kicked sand in his face, pushed him over, and made away with the pretty girl. At home the thin boy finally decided to subscribe to the advertised bodybuilding program. A few weeks later, he was sporting a new body with bulging muscles. Back on the beach with his girl, he stood up to the same sand-kicking tough guy and won the love of the pretty girl with one solid punch.

The Boy Scouts of America published a manual which taught not only how a be a good camper but also guidelines in healthy, clean living for young teenage boys. One paragraph in the book was subtitled "Conservation," and this was perplexing because we thought conservation dealt with forests, clean water, and things like that. But the text was directed towards good habits for a young man. We finally figured out, with some help from the older guys, the subject of this paragraph was masturbation. The book advised against it, but we were not sure exactly what we would be conserving.

The word got around that masturbation could make you sick, crazy, or very weak, and then there was the rumor that masturbation would make you blind. I figured if that was the case, I'd do it just until I needed glasses. Eventually the warnings about masturbation became a subject in our conversations.

"I think this stuff about jerking off is a lot of crap. My big brother told me that he's been doing it for years, and he's still strong enough to beat the shit of me."

Trying to be funny like my father, I said, "The only problem is that you don't meet any interesting people."

I was amazed at how easy I could become sexually aroused, and then how quickly an erection could fade away. I learned this in seventh grade math class where our teacher, while not particularly pretty, was physically well endowed. At that time, it was fashionable for women to wear very sheer, light, "see-through" blouses. I often sat in class staring at her blouse, fantasizing, and, at the same time, fearing that she would call me up to the board to work math problems, my protrusion in full view of the entire class.

We all had the same problem and dreaded a trip up to the blackboard. It was probably the only time in my life that I prayed for a non-erection.

I often wondered about our teacher. I noticed that she took a position at the window at an angle to the board where she could see our mid-sections no matter how we turned or squirmed.

Years later, on one occasion while undressing with a new, pretty date, I would picture teacher's "see-through" blouse wondering where that erection was now that I needed it.

Chapter 7

Nate left the slow-growing and poor-paying haberdashery business to become an insurance salesman/collector. In those days insurance premiums were paid as weekly collections to the salesman. Each day my father would make 10-12 visits to policyholders' homes.

He enjoyed good health in general, and, except for a nasty cold every winter and one other problem, rarely saw a doctor. The poor man was cursed with chronic constipation and had to take an enema every other night. His doctors did not object. In fact, one of the reasons that he lived to the age of 97 was that he probably was washed free of toxins. Every other night he would ask all of us if we had finished in the bathroom as he had to get in there to "move his furniture."

Nate

Nate's problem with chronic constipation was accompanied by a tendency for enormous amounts of gas. A plausible reason he shied away from office work. Being outdoors most the time was a blessing, although not always. On one occasion, he had one more call to make and he thought to himself, "Well, Mrs. Kane is almost always at home. I'll make a quick call and then head home."

He walked up to her porch, rang the bell and waited for her to appear. But there was no answer, so he rang again waited and waited.

"This is odd; she's almost always home and answers the door quickly. I'll try once more."

Still no answer, and, at this time, he felt the pressure of gas accumulating in his system. Giving up on her, he turned away pivoting on his left foot, raising his right leg, and releasing a clap of thunder that could be heard all over the neighborhood—some people reached for an umbrella. As if choreographed by Balanchine himself, the woman opened the door at that very instant.

"Excuse me; my shoes are too tight."

They both had a good laugh.

For Nate there was hardly a situation where a joke, a few laughs, and a good sense of humor failed to get him out of a tight spot. Whether it be a social setting, at home, or on the job, Nate was always ready to respond to people with a sense of humor. His smile and relaxed manner made people immediately comfortable in his presence. Along with his comedy, he always had an eye for a good-looking lady. He knew that his flirtations could someday lead to serious troubles but had little control over himself in this area. His rendezvous with an attractive new customer, Marianne, presented a novel and much different challenge.

A side benefit to Nate's new insurance job was the opportunity for new sexual adventures. The clients generally were women at home managing the household—often on a tight budget. Some would learn that weekly payments could easily be forgiven for a quick, convenient roll in the sack in the next room. It was expedient, and who would know?

❦ ❧

Marianne Marconi walked around her Brooklyn apartment viewing her newly arrived furniture from every possible angle. She was amazed at how the drab old look of her rooms were so much improved by a living room couch and a new dining room table in the kitchen. She had wanted modern furniture for a long time but waited for her husband John to insist on buying it.

"But, John, how are we ever going to pay for kitchen and living room furniture? We just barely get through the month," Marianne said.

"Sweetheart, with my new pay raise, we can do it. All we have to do is go downtown to Macy's, pick out the furniture, tell them that we'll pay for it over time and tell them where to deliver; it's that easy."

Her husband worked as both a waiter, chef, and assistant manager for a seafood restaurant in Sheep's Head Bay. He knew the business well and was such a hard worker that the owner relied on him frequently, sometimes over 10 hours a day, recently rewarding him with a big salary increase. John was very proud of his knowledge of the seafood business and didn't mind the long hours.

She had been thinking the same way and wanted to help pay for the modern furniture but had been unsuccessful at earning money. For some reason that she could not explain, whenever a job became just a little stressful or demanding, she would get nervous and hostile to coworkers. So she stayed home keeping busy with walks in Prospect Park, shopping on Flatbush Avenue, and occasional bowling with her girlfriends. She was bored most of the time, but for now her modern furniture kept her excited. She loved to run her hands over the silky, gold velour fabric that covered the sofa. The maple kitchen table matched the copper cooking utensils that hung from the kitchen wall. Her husband had insisted on copper and that was fine with her.

While they were in a spending mood, she took out a life insurance policy on her husband as her mother had been urging her to do for years. They bought the policy through a Prudential agent who was a frequent customer at the restaurant. She would pay the premium—about $.50 a week—from her household budget. An agent would call on her at home to collect.

She also decided to buy some new clothes including a couple of sweaters and a new skirt—all tight fitting. She had heard so much about the new cone-shaped *bullet* bra (*more like a torpedo in my case*, she thought) that was designed to keep a woman's breasts separated and projected. *The war is sure creeping into our lives*, she thought. Yes, it was time to buy a new bra.

Her mother always told her even as a young teenager, "Marianne you're going to have large beautiful breasts. At age 14 they are already big. Remember to always wear a good bra. If you want to meet a nice guy, remember to take care of God's gift."

Today was a special day for Marianne as the first insurance payment was due, and she was expecting a visit from the collection man. As she put on her new bullet bra she said to herself, "And now I shall stretch my new beautiful red sweater over these torpedoes. Oh, why am I getting so excited? Who knows, this man is probably an old fart who couldn't care less about me and my curves."

The door buzzer interrupted her thoughts, and she quickly ran over and opened the door.

"Hello, Mrs. Marconi. Let me introduce myself. I'm your new insurance agent, Nate Rubin."

Nate sat on the couch and watched Marianne as she carried ginger ale and cookies from the kitchen back to the living room. Without making it too obvious, his eyes soaked in the shape and movements of her curvaceous body. He couldn't help thinking about what some comedians would say in a situation like this.

"Don't you know, lady, it's not polite to point?" Or the comedian who upon meeting a Jane Russell shaped woman, put his mouth right up against or close to one of those conical-shaped projections, saying, "Hello, operator, give me long-distance."

These thoughts put a smile on his face which Marianne noticed much to her pleasure, as she thought, "Here is a remarkable man, good-looking with a respectable job, and he is happy and smiling while working. Maybe he can tell me why I am so uptight when I work. I wonder what his secret is, and, of course, I see him over there checking my boobs, but that's expected."

She sat down, and, as they started to drink ginger ale, she remarked, "What do you think of my modern furniture, Mr. Rubin? We just got it at Macy's, and it was delivered a few days ago. I just love it and can't stop touching it."

"You've got terrific taste, and I think this is the most comfortable sofa I ever sat on."

"I'm paying for it monthly with my husband's new raise and now with the insurance policy that's also a new expense for me. Which reminds me," she said, reaching out to hand him two quarters, "here is my first payment on the insurance policy."

"Listen, if your budget is tight this month, please understand that we're not in a big rush to collect your money. We just want to have a good relationship with you and want you to feel good about the company."

She listened and thought to herself, "Wow, I think this guy has fallen for me like a cannonball. Well, that's okay and I think he's a pretty cute guy too."

During the subsequent two visits, they talked and joked and enjoyed each other's company. Getting ready to leave on his third visit, he thought he could be a little bold lowering his face close to her breasts and jokingly saying, "Hello, operator, I'm calling for long-distance."

She laughed out loud and grabbed him by both ears and pulled him in very close while both leaned against the door. He composed himself, opened the door, then said, "Goodbye, Marianne; see you next week."

Walking down the stairs, he felt that special warm, awakened feeling that usually accompanied the gradual bulging in his trousers.

Marianne Marconi and Nate felt a certain chemistry for each other and they looked forward to their weekly visits. They quickly discovered that they had one very big interest in common and that was professional football.

"You mean that you're a football fan? What a surprise, a delightful surprise. You're the first woman I've ever met who likes football. Most women find it a pain in the neck."

"I grew up in Chicago during a period when the Bears were one of the best teams in the country. My father and brothers were all lovers of football. I guess I just joined in with them. I got to really like it and the Chicago Bears were special."

"I'm a New Yorker, but I'll never forget the 1940 Championship game with the Chicago Bears; it must have been a great thrill for you."

"Beating the Redskins by 71 points was unbelievable."

"Brooklyn had a pretty good year too, and what about Ace Parker?"

Nate

His visits were short. Each time they sat closer interrupting their conversation with touching, kissing, and staring into each other's eyes. They naturally found their way into the bedroom. He was fascinated by the unusual shape of her bra and soon overwhelmed by the size and shape of her breasts. She seemed slightly embarrassed as the extra weight that she had put on recently caused him to tug hard to pull her panties over her waist. They made love in a hurry holding each other tightly until they were both exhausted. He would look at his watch while she held onto him; then she would let go knowing that he had many calls to make that day.

"Oh, Nate, you make me feel so good. I have never experienced anything this wonderful," she said stroking him and kissing him. "Maybe it's because you're an insurance man…."

He interrupted her. "That's exactly what this is about. It's the Rock of Gibraltar. You've seen the Rock on all our papers and envelopes. Yes, we are a bunch of rock-hard men.

"In fact, Marianne, I must tell you something. When we first got into bed I thought to myself, 'is this all for me?'"

"Oh, Nate, you are such a funny guy, and, in fact, that brings me to a subject that I wanted to talk to you about," she added, her tone becoming serious. "I am about ready to tell my husband that I'm leaving him because I want to spend the rest of my life with you, Nate."

Nate jumped up out of bed and began to quickly dress himself while using as many words as he could find to throw ice on this idea. She listened and only stared.

Nate was facing the consequence that he knew was inevitable. For a married man having an extramarital affair, the problem was not like solving the Riddle of the Sphinx. It was as simple as having your cake and eating it. The real issue was when and how it ends.

The following week he entered her apartment only to find her irate husband waiting for him.

"You goddamn Jew bastard. How dare you break up my family? I'll get you for this. Yes, I'll sue your ass and your company as well."

They did indeed bring a lawsuit against the insurance company and Nate the agent for alienation of affection. She claimed that she and Nate had spent many hours talking about their love for each other and their future life together. Fortunately, the insurance company lawyer was able to show that this was a lie. The company had collection data that showed that each visit to her was followed with at least seven more calls, and then my mother confirmed he was home for dinner by 6:30. It was impossible for anything to have occurred beyond the physical act (i.e., wham bam, thank you ma'am).

Nate won the lawsuit but lost his job. Fortunately, at that time the country was in the process of building its war machine.

CRACK!! She swung the broom at him, missing and hitting a kitchen chair.

"What the hell is wrong with you! You're not a single man free to mess around. You have a family to worry about," she yelled, red faced and eyes bulging. "Where the hell are you going to get a job now?"

Dora felt like she had been hit by a cannon ball. Disappointed and frustrated, an image of her first husband's face raced through her mind. "Why should I have such bad luck?" she said shaking her head.

This was a question she would ask herself many times in the future. Eventually she would turn to religion and to God for answers or at least for comfort and peace of mind, which she indeed would find but only through her children.

Chapter 8

News of the Japanese attack on Pearl Harbor interrupted our radio program that Sunday night. My parents discussed the attack for hours, and I remember the worried look on their faces. The full meaning and scope of the war came to me and my friends gradually through the movies. We saw John Wayne, machine gun in one hand, grenade in the other leading his men under fire toward the enemy. Movies like this gave us a clear picture of the killing and destructive side of war, and it entered our play with improvised guns and trenches as we dealt with the enemy in our own way. With one of my best friends, we lined up chairs in our kitchens and sat in the cockpit of a torpedo plane searching for Japanese ships.

Our teachers at school seemed to understand the powerful effect the war had on our picture of life. In art class, for example, we drew aircraft carriers and fighter planes overhead in dogfights with Japanese zeros. My teacher occasionally would comment, "Can't you boys think of anything else to draw?"

Everyone adjusted to wartime living. Things that we were accustomed to and took for granted were no longer in the stores. Our favorite candies and bubblegum disappeared replaced by awful-tasting replacements. Each home was given a ration book with stamps to buy soap, meat, and butter. There was a shortage of fat and sugar which were needed for the war effort—fat for explosives and candy for the troops.

Nate applied for an inspection job at one of the aircraft companies on Long Island. He had to pass a test involving some geometry. My sister tried to help him but threw up her hands in frustration. She later told me that he did not know even the simplest concepts. His distaste for school and studies became clear. I listened and hid my disappointment by mentally blaming my sister as he did.

Nate was hired by Republic Aviation on Long Island, where the Thunderbolt fighter/bomber was manufactured. The Thunderbolt, a light and fast bomber, played a vital role behind the scenes in taking out enemy troop trains and ammunition storage. My friends were in awe of me after learning that my father was working on the Thunderbolt and that one of these days he was going to bring home some shells from the test firing range.

Nate became an Air Raid Warden, and, when the air raid siren started, he put on his helmet, armband, and gas mask and left the darkened house to go into the darkened streets where I could barely hear his voice.

I was very proud of his contributions to the war effort, although I never actually saw him do anything in action.

My mother contributed as well. One lady on our block was receiving letters from her soldier son who was fighting overseas. Since she could not read English, she brought her letters to my mother, who translated them into Yiddish. The lady cried, worried about her son, and this gave me a good taste of how families had been broken up with sons and daughters leaving for the service and for faraway countries. The heartbreak of the war came even closer as I learned the meaning of the Gold Stars hanging in the windows of my neighborhood.

At school we were taught the meaning of patriotism and that together we would win this war. I was selected to carry the American flag flanked by student honor guards at school assembly. We would wait in the wings for the music to start and then march down the aisle and then back up, placing the American flag and the New York State flag in their proper holders as the assembly sang:

I'd like to be the sort of man the flag can boast about;

I'd like to be the sort of man it cannot live without;

I'd like to be the type of man

That really is American:

The head erect and shoulders square,

Clean minded fellow, just and fair

That all men picture when they see

The glorious banner of the free.

And

We're all for one and one for all,

Clinging together like the ivy on the garden wall.

All for one and one for all—

Best of friends are we, jolly good company.

We keep singing this song to help us on our way,

Never mind tomorrow—it's a lovely day today.

We're all for one and one for all and altogether we can't go wrong.

For my mother years of being broke financially and the episode with Marianne pulled her downward, and the resulting sadness seemed to go directly to her eyes. At least that's the impression I had, and, as I lost faith in my father, I prayed that she would have a long life. We had hoped she would reach 100, but she only made it to 99.

Even as a young boy, I had seen that sadness and somehow felt the responsibility to love her enough to compensate for whatever it was that was making her so miserable. As the years passed, I came to realize that her melancholy was based on her disappointment in my father, whom I admired and loved so much. The structure of school along with the challenge of making good grades became my great escape.

Meanwhile my mother independently dealt with her sadness, and this led her along a path of religious awakening.

Chapter 9

The end of the war brought a conclusion to Nate's defense job and the start of a yearlong search for a steady, reliable job to support his family. He searched mainly for sales work because he thought of himself principally as a salesman. Unfortunately, he never finished high school, and the market was flooded with service men returning to civilian life. As a routine he would scour the want ads, answer one or two, and come home discouraged and disappointed. He talked quietly about his failure to my mother and then went off to the couch with the newspaper.

I took this hiatus seriously as I became acutely aware of his shortcomings as a provider. My image of him as a young athlete remained but not without a few questions. I had seen many signs of his abilities, but he did not participate in sports now. His life was limited to work and the newspaper. His inability to find work was another blow to the image I had of this man whom I had always loved and admired. Nevertheless, I propped him up mentally and was happy that he was my father and that he was always ready to clown around with us. I did not show my unhappiness to my parents. Secretly I saw my family as a ship that was damaged and taking on water. A hidden camera would reveal a sad and worried family and a depressed mother.

༄ ༅

Nate started thinking about the idea of owning his own business, getting away from bosses and low salaries, hiring and firing. He quickly jumped at an opportunity that came up in our neighborhood.

The grocery store around the corner was put up for sale by the elderly couple who owned and had run it for many years. They told my father that it was small enough to operate alone yet big enough to earn his family a good living. Nate and Dora went to friends and relatives to borrow the $7000 needed to buy the store and its stock. Back in those days, they referred to the entire store property as "lock, stock, and barrel."

The previous owners spent a week training Nate, and then he was left on his own without any prior experience. Dora was helpful in teaching him about some of the grocery products. He had never shopped or spent much time in the kitchen. His weak back was to become the worst problem. He ended up in bed during the first week on his own with a severe backache from bending and lifting. Putting canned goods up on the shelf was no easy task, but the real challenge came with milk deliveries. Milk was delivered and left on the sidewalk in front of the store in heavy reinforced wooden crates, nine bottles in each. Milk was sold in glass deposit bottles that the customer returned to the store and which Nate had to return to the delivery truck. The store received about nine of these crates every few days. He loaded them onto a dolly about two or three at a time, wheeled them into the store, and then loaded the bottles into the display refrigerator. These steps were brutally tough on his weak back and disheartening since there was only about a penny profit per bottle.

My sister was a young teenager at the time and was able to come in after school to help. He also had help from a young high school boy named Murray Stern who did some stock work and deliveries. The store had a delivery bicycle designed with a shortened front wheel, making room for a large wire basket mounted above. Murray was strong and able to help, but he had a mean sense of humor and liked to embarrass my sister. One afternoon when I happened to be hanging out at the store, he poured heavy cream onto a piece of wax paper, came out of the stock room, and showed it to my sister telling her that he had just masturbated. She screamed at him, but he only laughed it off as playful fun.

The Chinese laundry was located around the corner from the grocery store, and the proprietor, a short middle-age Chinese man with a strong build and a slight smile on his face, was able to make several trips a day to pick up milk, rice, and occasionally a can of tuna fish.

Nate was very interested in this man since as a boy the Chinese in his neighborhood were teased and humiliated whenever they were in sight. This man looked as friendly as most of his customers, so Nate finally struck up a conversation.

"Hello, sir, my name is Nate Rubin, and, as you probably know, I took over the store a couple months ago."

"Yes, hello, my name is Sam Lee and I know that you are new here. I wish you best of luck. I own the laundry around the corner, Sam Lee Laundry."

"I am very curious about Chinese laundries," offered Nate. Why do you call them Chinese laundry? Is that because you have a unique way of cleaning clothes—maybe something you learned back in your old country?"

"No, no, we clean clothes the same way everybody does—wash, rinse, wring out, hang to dry, and maybe iron," he responded in a soft voice. "We say Chinese laundry today, but it started maybe 100 years ago. Many Chinese people come to this country. They had no skills, no way to get decent job. Americans don't like Chinese. Make life very tough. Same time many Americans here in New York or even in California make more money; economy good. Many American ladies want to pay someone to do laundry. No one likes to clean the clothes. In the big cities like New York, apartments were very small and crowded. Not too much room to do laundry. Chinese immigrants began to wash and iron laundry day and night week after week—not an effortless way to earn a living but it was the only way available to the Chinese.

"Soon Chinese joined together and opened stores, so people bring laundry to the store. Chinese work hard—12 to15 hours every day—making clothes very clean and folded nice. But make lots of money. Laundries open all over country even St. Louis. Everybody calls laundries 'Chinese laundry.'

"Laundry business very tough," Sam Lee commented to Nate as he showed him his hands—dry, wrinkled, and rough from handling wet clothes with strong laundry soap.

Nate

"Yes, I know about working hard. My tough job here is carrying those heavy crates of milk. I also know that the Chinese were given a very tough time here. I think all minorities are hated or at least mistrusted here in this country. You see I am Jewish, and Jews have not been accepted completely either."

A few weeks went by. Nate and Sam exchanged small talk on his visits to the store; they formed a certain bond perhaps because they each owned a small business and each was a minority. This friendship grew over a period of months and one day Sam offered an invitation to Nate.

"Please come to my apartment and have dinner with my family and bring your wife and children. My apartment is up the stairs above the laundry."

Nate accepted the invitation and they settled on a date and time.

Nate and family arrived at Sam's apartment full of curiosity and anticipation. Sam introduced his wife and two small children, and we sat down to eat; the dinner table was so small that some of us held our bowls of rice in our laps.

Nate tried to stimulate some dinner table conversation. "When we were young kids, we thought that Confucius was God to the Chinese and this was their religion. We quoted many of

Confucius's sayings—some of them very funny, some very dirty or mean. What I really am so curious about is do you pray to Confucius? Is that your religion?"

Unwittingly, Nate had struck a favorite note with Sam Lee who, while not a very religious man, was a serious student of Confucius.

"No, not a religion and not a God. As a young man, Confucius worked for the government, but he was restless because he did not agree with their ways. He traveled to different states trying to reform but not successful. As an older man, he became a teacher, and this is what he loved best."

"What subjects did he like to teach?"

"I don't know what subjects you would call it today—maybe philosophy, maybe psychology. His main interest was relationships among people. He had an idea of a superior individual, a wise man like a sage but who was also righteous with a kind, human heart."

"That sounds a lot like the *tzadik* or righteous man that the Jewish people talk a lot about," Dora said, pleased to find something in common. "The tzadik is a man who tries to do the right thing all of the time. Is that what Confucius was referring to also?"

Nate

"Yes, it is similar, and Confucius taught that by seeking the good, those who followed this sage would also be good."

The conversation at the table turned to the food served as Dora was quite interested in the shape and flavor of some of the vegetables served. She had eaten in the Chinese restaurant several blocks away but didn't find anything quite the same at the Lee table. The Lees explained that the food at the Chinese restaurant is not true Chinese but really an imitation and may be designed for Western taste.

Dora was quite impressed as she observed a kind of smooth, easy-going relationship between Sam and his wife and their two children. "Your children are so relaxed and well behaved. Did Confucius teach you about how to raise children?"

"Confucius taught that everyone owes a duty to his superiors, and, at the same time, has a responsibility toward his inferiors. This means that the parent is responsible for his child while the child owes obedience to the parent; the husband is responsible to his wife while the wife owes a duty of obedience to her husband. This type of relationship is for everyone and leads to an ordered society."

Dora silently related this idea to her own life—to some of her confusions and disappointments.

She felt sad thinking about her own marriage, and then she quickly turned her attention to the chopsticks she was learning to use, then put them down to help her children with theirs.

School was my savior. The teachers and principal found ways to elevate me and make me feel special. On one memorable day, my teacher called two of my classmates and me to her desk and announced, "You three have been selected to visit the principal in her office because you have scored the very highest in the recent three-day tests that you have taken. Be sure to tell your parents all about this."

My mother suffered frustration and worry at Nate's business failures, and I was getting particularly adept at reading the signs in her eyes—a slight squint, the beginning of a cry, a faraway look as if observing an event many miles away. Our grocery business lasted about one year. The supermarket was a new concept in the retail grocery business. Purchasing goods in large, low-cost quantities gave supermarkets an advantage in offering attractive prices to the budget conscious consumer. The objective was to sell and turnover the inventory quickly, creating enough cash flow to continue the process. The small neighborhood grocery could not compete with the new low prices. Nate's customers came to him now only for the convenience of buying milk and dairy products—the very products that represented backbreaking work and little profit. Nate and his financers failed to read the tea leaves.

There was good news on the horizon for her as she was going to be blessed in March with a little baby girl, a happy, beautiful, laughing child who was to bring immense pleasure to a late in life mother badly in need of such a blessing.

I first learned about this the previous fall on a trip to Cape Cod, where my Aunt Rose had a cottage near the beach. While I was excited about this trip, I worried about a slight problem. I had grown out of bedwetting a few years earlier but was concerned that the problem could reappear any time especially in a strange bed. My mother reminded me, "If you wake with the urge to go while you're in bed, call me and I'll walk you out to the bathroom." That didn't happen.

I woke up that morning about 5:30 in a great panic because the bed was soaking wet. Everyone in the family would discover what I'd done, and I would be humiliated.

Being the resourceful young man that I was, I decided to take advantage of the deep closet in that bedroom, so I peeled the wet sheets away from the bed, rolled them into a tight bundle, and pushed them as far back in the closet as I could.

Barbara had been a live-in maid with my aunt since the time she was orphaned as a young girl of about 12 or 13. She had become part of the family. Later that morning I heard her exclaim to my aunt, "I'm sure that I put sheets on that bed."

That night when I went to bed, I found that fresh dry linen had been placed on the bed and the wet sheets had been removed from the closet. My crime had been discovered; now I awaited punishment. And to my surprise I never heard about it. I guess they figured that the event was more than enough of a punishment.

On the way home, we stopped in Quincy to visit my Aunt May (my mother had four sisters and one brother) and my Uncle Art, who was like my father in many ways and a lot of fun to be around. He had a deep voice and spoke with clear distinct diction. Like Nate he had a keen sense of humor.

"Now young man, when you get home tonight, tell your father that you went to the picture show here and that the movie you saw was *Rivka's Tuchus in Two Parts.*"

"Sounds like you have been hanging around your Uncle Art" was Nate's comment that night.

Nate

Riding home on the train that day, I learned that in about six months I would be getting a little baby sister or brother.

All my relatives and all our neighbors on my block were surprised and even shocked. We were a family quite settled in size in everyone's eyes. This addition was hard for people to imagine at first, but as Dora grew our neighbors got used to the idea and shared in the excitement.

My older sister at age 16 was so embarrassed she was afraid to walk up our street. "Oh, mother, how could you do this to me," she exclaimed.

Chapter 10

"Honestly, Dora, I have often wondered how Jews can get along without the belief and faith that we have in our Lord Jesus Christ. I've never shared these thoughts with anyone else. To be sure I don't know what I would do without my faith. This cross around my neck reminds me of how Jesus, through my faith in him, brings me salvation, and that's not only for the life after but in my everyday life here on earth. He is with me, he supports me, and he assures me that everything will be okay."

Mother, in response, said, "I went to a church service one time and part of a hymn that I remember said, 'He walks with me and he talks with me.' Is that what you mean?"

"Yes, that's exactly it. But what brought you to a church service?"

And so went a typical conversation between my mother and one of her best friends, Joyce

O'Connor, an Irish Catholic whose family had settled in New York during the potato famine. My mother had several good Christian friends, and she often got into conversations with them about religion.

She had sensed in her Christian friends a sincere belief in Jesus Christ which brought with it the benefit of a mystical support that helped make life's tragedies and disappointments a lot easier to bear. She was increasingly envious of that quality as her disappointments, especially my father, began to mount over the years. She was not one to simply accept things as they are but rather to try to get what you want, which in this case was peace of mind and emotional support. She got this mental drive from her father who made a living in the old country in their small town about 50 miles east of Kraków where he was a taxicab driver bringing people from the train station to the wonderful warm water spa about 10 miles outside of town. In this way he saved enough money to bring his family including two children to the United States where he became a baker and eventually built up a bakery with delivery trucks. At the dinner table, I had heard that his six children sat frightened and in strict obedience of him. My recollection of him on the few times that I visited was that he had a very strong personality, but I am happy to say that he liked me.

So, as time allowed, my mother pursued the history of Christianity and the life and teachings of Jesus and the Jewish religion as it existed during that time.

As I learned from overhearing her conversations with friends, while her pursuit was mainly an intellectual endeavor, she had a deep-seated desire to understand why there were two religions and not one. After all, Jesus was a Jew. If all of the teachings back then had been combined back into one religion, today she could be enjoying the best of all thinking and ideas.

I listened quietly as she related her newfound insights to Joyce.

"The turning point for the Jews who were widely spread about the Roman Empire, living mostly in peace, came in the fourth century when Emperor Constantine initiated the establishment of Christianity as the official religion of the Roman Empire.

"Why would he have taken on such an enormous task?"

"He had a mystical experience in which, in a dream, he saw his sword change into a cross. The next day, terribly outnumbered, he went into battle and emerged miraculously victorious. He attributed his victory to his dream where the cross of Jesus had appeared to him as an omen. In addition, his mother, who was influential in his life, had converted to Christianity some years earlier."

"Why do you say that it was a turning point?"

"Constantine brought the Christian leaders together to establish among other things the dogma of the religion. This group decided that Jesus was not a separate human being but rather was in a mystical way part of the God of the Old Testament, the God the Jews had worshiped thousands of years. This appeared to be a breakaway from the strict monotheism so basic to the Jewish religion. Unfortunately, this distinction became and remained the basis for Jewish reluctance to convert to Christianity."

"I can understand Constantine's challenge in converting pagans to Christianity, especially considering the enormous size of the pagan world, but I can't see why it was important to him to convert the Jews who were after all a small minority." Joyce said.

"It was the pagans who resisted and argued strongly saying that there were many like Jesus who made the same claims to similar teachings and miracles. They asserted that Jesus was just another among many.

Constantine had a very strong argument, though, which ultimately convinced most of the pagan world. He argued that Jesus came from the Jews who had a history and tradition of thousands of years, a *Bible*, a nation, and, most importantly, a prophecy in their tradition that almost word for word predicted the coming of Jesus."

"So Constantine was a clever guy, but why did that become a problem for the Jews?"

"The fact that the Jews would not convert was an embarrassment. The picture was totally inconsistent. If this man of Jewish heritage claimed that he was the true son of God, it would only be natural for the Jews to follow Him, but they didn't, and that was a problem for Constantine and for the church leaders who followed."

Chapter 11

"Dora, you seem to be so much sadder today. Are you feeling depressed? I thought that with the baby coming you would feel so much happier," Joyce said offering a sympathetic ear.

"Joyce, I am extremely worried. Nate just can't seem to find a job. We have no income; the future doesn't look good. I just don't feel good about bringing a new baby into such an insecure future."

Pounding her fist on the table, my mother released some pent-up anger. "I hate to say this, but my husband is nothing more than an inept clown."

"We have always liked him so much—all of us, my husband, my kids," Joyce replied trying to understand. "I think you're telling me something about your life that I never imagined."

My mother took a moment to dry her eyes and regain some composure. "It's not just the money side of this. He just doesn't seem to care; he's oblivious to problems and situations that are difficult. I seem to be the only one capable of dealing with problems. He couldn't even put a can opener on the wall. He's not at all involved in my kids' lives. He seems to know so little about running a house or about everyday things that we all deal with. Let me give you a couple of examples of the incredible stupidity that I live with.

"We keep our radio on top of the refrigerator. One night he wanted to move it to another room, but he couldn't reach the wire plug that hangs down behind the refrigerator. So he tried pry out the plug from the outlet with a butter knife. He quickly received an electrical shock that threw him across the room. Nobody in this world except Nate would stick a butter knife into an electrical socket."

Once again, she wiped the perspiration and tears from her face. "I'm ashamed to tell you about this one, Joyce, but it's true and shows how there's something wrong with this man. Driving one day, I started to smell what I thought was dog doo. I've known for a long time that if a dog leaves a pile somewhere in the neighborhood somehow Nate will step in it. So I pulled over to the curb and asked him to check the bottom of his shoes. Instead of taking his shoe off to look at it, he leaned over and ran his index finger along the bottom of the shoe. He came up with his index finger covered with dog shit."

Joyce shook her head in amazement. "Dora, I've always had so much fun around him, but the more I think about it, the more I see what you mean. There's a kind of sadness and self-deprecation in his humor. He reminds me in many ways of Charlie Chaplin."

"Yes, indeed it is sad. And the sadness runs even deeper. He lives for that damn newspaper and takes no interest in his family. And now he can't find a job. It's just dragging me down."

Looking directly at Joyce she said, "I know you have had your troubles too. And, yet, you seem so content. Is it your faith that seems to hold you up? I envy the sense of security that your religion and your Savior give you."

"You are a remarkable woman, Dora. Of all the Jewish women I've known, none have had the interest in Jesus and Christianity that you have. Sometimes I wonder if you are seriously thinking about converting to Christianity."

"Joyce, I don't think I could ever do such a thing. It's an enormous step and my father would kill me. I do think about your personal Savior though. Your faith in Jesus seems to support you so much."

"I think you should go and talk to my priest, Father Murphy. He's a kind and sympathetic man. No need for a long session; just sit with him and tell him everything that's on your mind."

"Maybe I will, Joyce; maybe I will do it for you. And if I feel guilty about it, I'll blame it on you."

"Dora, you should give up this guilt stuff." Joyce smiled at her.

As she walked down the main aisle of the church, she sensed a tremendous space overhead, bigger than anything she had ever seen in a synagogue. This space appeared to be filled by hundreds of stained glass squares lit by the afternoon sun, forming a vast array of dazzling colors. She walked slowly while looking around. Her footsteps were muffled by the soft carpeting. There was an unfamiliar odor here and she wondered if they were burning incense or had they burned it so many times it was absorbed by the furniture and walls. As she approached the altar, details of a large crucifix became clear. She began to feel her heart pounding. Is this what God really looks like, she wondered. Or is this what the son of God really looks like? That's what they believe. She felt that she was in a holy place and maybe in the presence of God but quickly was overtaken by a sense of guilt, a sense of being out of place, not belonging, and a fear of punishment that she knew so well since childhood.

"Good afternoon, Dora," the priest said interrupting her thoughts. "I hope you don't mind me calling you by your first name. I'm Father Murphy. This was a clever idea for us to meet here in the pews where we can be relaxed rather than in my office." His voice was calm and peaceful. He appeared to be a little overweight with a small white beard and a large red nose. She was amused by the thought that he could be Chris Kringle posing as a priest.

She spoke quietly. Her first impulse was to explain her mental situation and then leave quickly, but his warm smile and his kind eyes put her at ease, and she even wondered briefly if priests like this are used to soften up Jews into conversion.

He, in fact, had no strong impulse to push the idea of conversion. He was attracted to this good-looking woman with her natural ability to interact with such complete attention.

"Dora, this need for—let's call it emotional support—that you feel so strongly is something that I am quite familiar with. You see, our Lord Jesus Christ recognized that the Jews of his time were strongly oppressed and persecuted by the Romans. They urgently wanted political and military action against Rome. But they had a much more basic personal need that I would call peace of mind. In His ministry here on Earth, He talked about private prayer at home. He often referred to his Father, the Jewish God, as a child would refer to his daddy. His was a very personal approach to religion and God; for example, we can pray quietly and alone. The offer of salvation simply through faith in Him was within easy reach of everybody."

She responded, "I understand His personal appeal. It's hard to believe that His approach to religion was rejected as they rejected and destroyed Him. But conversion for me seems like a major and almost impossible step."

"Dora, I have met many Jewish people with similar conflicts and have come to a few conclusions. Judaism offers a strong bond to God through adherence to His commandments. It's a wonderful feeling to know that you are following God's laws through the traditions of Judaism. Many Jews feel safe and secure in this way. The attempts by the church to convert Jews have been futile because for thousands of years they have found great peace in following the commandments of their one true God."

He paused and looked into her eyes. "On the other hand, for those relatively few Jews who, through faith, have accepted Jesus Christ as their Savior, I have seen stress and inner conflict disappear, replaced by a deep sense of peace." He reached out with a warm smile.

"I wish you Godspeed in your search."

Chapter 12

"My meeting with your priest reminded me of some things I learned about Martin Luther when I took a short course in the origins of anti-Semitism. Early in his ministry around the year 1520, Luther wrote that the Catholic Church was taking the wrong approach to converting the Jews. They were too rough and threatening. He would be more rational and deal gently in the conversion process. He was optimistic and very complimentary."

"But he wasn't too successful, was he?"

"No, he failed and was very disappointed. His writings toward the end of his ministry around 1540 tried to explain his failure. He could only say that Jews were under the control of the devil. Jewish stubbornness had an evil source. Many people have believed that such criticism of the Jews by Martin Luther, who was responsible for the Protestant Reformation, was the origin of hundreds of years of anti-Semitism and persecution of the Jews in Europe."

"Dora, do you believe that so much hatred should be placed on his shoulders?"

"No, I don't think so. It's a factor though and possibly an important one. But I'm so happy to say that the Austrian Evangelical Lutheran Church in 1998 formally accepted responsibility for much of the anti-Semitism and, most importantly, proclaimed respect for the Jewish community today. This new joining of hands was based on common beliefs, traditions, and heritage. In a sense they were saying that arguments about the differences in the two religions have led nowhere. I think I heard similar ideas from your priest."

She smiled warmly at Joyce. "I am developing a lot of innovative ideas about my religion." She paused then added, "For example, I realize that I pray to the same God that Jesus prayed to."

A few weeks later on a gusty March morning, my friends and I gathered around a large taxicab as it arrived in front of my house. My mother and father emerged with a tiny little package wrapped tightly in warm blankets. We stood in awe. My street in Brooklyn would never be the same.

Now I saw my mother walk with confidence and pride knowing that she was living her life in accordance with what God expected of her, and in return she would treasure this very precious gift from Him.

My sister came relatively late in life but not too late to bring our mother immeasurable joy.

Chapter 13

Nate's job at the aircraft company ended at a time when millions of men were returning from overseas looking for work. These men were given preference and rightfully so.

Nate's job prospects look grim, but he never lost his sense of humor and we continued to laugh at him. At one New Year's Eve party for the family at our home, he took the ice bucket and tongs and went around urging people to let him remove their hemorrhoids. Only he could pull off a stunt like that and make it hilariously funny.

To my mother, who also laughed at his antics, the nightmare of how to feed and clothe the family and pay the rent was back after a one-year reprieve.

Nate's sister Sylvia was married to a man from Washington, D.C., who had inherited his father's insurance business. They had a young son and lived in a large apartment on Connecticut Avenue.

Sylvia called one day and said, "I'm wondering if you and Dora would be willing to pick up and move to Washington because the insurance business is doing pretty good, and I think that Joe could find a pretty good spot for you."

Pleased to hear about such an opportunity, Nate answered with a big smile. "Sounds interesting but don't you think I would want to try it out before we move the family to D.C.?"

"Apartments here are extremely scarce and that situation will continue for about a year, so I think it will work out best if you come live with Joe and me and make trips home on the train every month or so."

"Are you sure you've got room for me?"

"Don't worry; we'll figure something out. Jump on a train down here real soon."

I missed Nate terribly during those periods of a month or two when he was away. My only compensation was the excitement and thrill of moving to the capital. I had a travel book with pictures of all the monuments and looked at them when I felt sad. I told all my friends that I was moving to Washington. I felt important and proud.

After about a year, my father came home announcing that he wasn't going back. Joe was missing without any warning. The company's cash assets were depleted. No one could explain his disappearance.

After about a month of searching, the police discovered that he was on a merchant Marine ship making stops all over the world. He had been having an affair with a woman in Washington, had fathered a child, and was trapped into paying her great sums of money.

Joe returned a few years later and was able to put his life together again. With the money he had saved over the years that he was away, he purchased a small paint business and moved to Florida with my aunt and their young son.

Chapter 14

Dora was raised in Binghamton, New York, the fourth of five children. Yiddish was spoken at home, so she was bilingual as an adult. Her parents studied English at city schools, but the demands of work and family made progress quite slow. With her wavy black hair and dark eyes, she was the prettiest of the four girls. She studied piano and made good grades at school. She was an appealing teenage girl and attracted boys at school as well as the men who hung around the butcher, where she shopped for her mother.

Two of Dora's four sisters, Anna and Sarah, were born in Poland and accompanied my grandparents as they immigrated to the United States in around 1905. In Poland grandfather Jacob made a better than average living with a horse drawn carriage carrying passengers from the train station in Tarnow to a beautiful hot springs spa located outside of their town. Working hard, he met as many trains as possible, charged a fair price, and, in a few years, saved enough money to bring his wife and tiny children to the United States.

They settled in Binghamton, New York, a city at that time of about 40,000 located in southern upstate New York at the junction of the Susquehanna and Chenango Rivers in a valley at the foothills of the Catskill Mountains. As with most of the immigrants coming to the United States, he was attracted by economic opportunities. In the early 1900s, due to a major expansion in shoe manufacturing (Endicott Johnson), Binghamton became one of the fastest growing cities in the United States. With an abundance of manufacturing jobs, Binghamton attracted thousands of immigrants from Italy and Eastern Europe—certainly not because of the weather since the area experienced some of the highest levels of rainfall and snow in the country. Binghamton was damp and cold.

While he had no interest in manufacturing, Jacob saw an opportunity to offer freshly-baked bread and cakes based upon favorite recipes from the old world. He and Becky, my grandmother, baked the rich traditional challah bread for neighboring families to celebrate the end of the Sabbath on Saturday evenings. They would prepare several loaves on Friday that they wrapped in towels to maintain freshness. The synagogue was about 300 yards from their home, so they were able to walk home after services to bring the bread back for the congregation. They had both learned the secrets of baking wonderful bread from their parents, most important of which was the quality and freshness of the ingredients. In his travels to the train station and spa, Jacob had the advantage of passing some of the best farms and wheat mills in that part of Poland.

In time he built a bakery business with a retail store and deliveries to local grocery stores. As he had predicted, his selection of recipes and the use of only high-quality ingredients, low in sugar and salt, led to an appealing variety of baked goods that were appreciated and demanded by the local citizens.

Just as his business expanded, Jacob's family grew and filled up their home adjacent to the bakery. Dora, her two younger sisters, and her brother were born and raised in Binghamton, and, as their size allowed, shared in the running of the bakery.

The family prospered, and the children grew. Anna married Joe Goodman a handsome articulate young man, and a little later Sarah married Sam Klein, a strong muscular man who grew up on a local dairy farm. Joe and Dora's brother Isaac took on a major share of the arduous work in running a bakery, and Joe drove the delivery truck to the retail stores scattered in the area.

Bored with the daily routine of the business, Isaac was always searching for new and better products to diversify. The news of the wonderful donuts that had become so popular in Europe reached welcome ears. Acting on some of his father's creativity and entrepreneurship, Isaac sectioned off a little area in the bakery to experiment with various flours, oils, and sugar and methods of shaping the dough and frying them at the right temperature in the best oil. His challenging work paid off with the opening of a little shop in downtown Binghamton, where a passerby could watch with fascination as donuts were formed and cooked as they floated in hot oil. The delicious aroma of freshly cooked donuts lured the crowds that gathered into the shop to sample this new delicacy. Donuts became Isaac's life work and in later years contributed to the Dunkin' Donuts concept.

My grandfather's business prospered for many years up until the time when he could no longer stand for long hours because his feet were sore and swollen from diabetes. He announced his retirement and his plan to leave the business to his son to be shared with both sons-in-law. Sam claimed and rightfully so that he had worked harder than the others, and therefore was entitled to a bigger share. As son of the owner of the business, Isaac contended that lawfully he should inherit the business. He argued that Sam was by nature a hard-working, strong man and that his challenging work in the bakery was as natural for him as getting up in the morning with the chickens. At the same time, Anna and Sarah as daughters of the owner demanded their legacy rights. The final decision was in Jacob's hands. Being a fair-minded man, he recognized and sympathized with all the claims including his two daughters whom he loved dearly. He wanted all of them to have a good future and to have an equitable share in the business. Unfortunately, after many months of arguing and fighting, the three men could not resolve the problem of how to divide up the business. The business was sold and the proceeds divided among three children.

With his share Sam bought a grocery store which, based on location and size, had terrific potential.

Joe earned a real estate license and began his own agency. With continued business momentum and new government contracts to supply World War II fighting men, the real estate business prospered. The population of Binghamton doubled in the early 1940s. Uncle Joe took on the face of a successful businessman, wearing fine suits and smoking expensive cigars, always bragging about Binghamton as if he were a member of the Chamber of Commerce.

Generally, based on their extra years of experience, older sisters have a way of taking their younger siblings by the hand and guiding them to a smoother, better path in life. This was particularly true for Dora's sisters who admired Dora even as children and young adults because she was so much fun and was the only one who had learned to play the piano and entertained the family with music. It was well known that Dora was much better looking than her sisters, and we don't know how this factored into their future relationships, but it was well recognized that her older sisters loved and cared for Dora and could empathize with the situations that she encountered—first with her divorce and in later years her situation with Nate, who could not settle into a new job in New York. They found as they talked to Dora on the telephone, another opportunity to reach out to help solve her problems like older sisters are prone to do. As the oldest and with a husband who was a successful real estate agent, Anna offered a practical solution.

"Dora, I think you should move your family to Binghamton. First, because it's a better quality of life. There is so much crime and Mafia now in Brooklyn— not a good place to raise a family. Nate will have a terrific future working in Joe's real estate business. Of course, in the beginning he will go door-to-door trying to find listings of people who want to buy or sell. Someone with more selling experience will follow up. Believe me it only takes one sale a month for Nate to bring home enough money for your family. In the future, as he learns the business he will get a license, become a real estate salesman, and do very well."

Sarah, while also encouraging her sister to come to Binghamton with her family, was a little more cautious and, like her hard-working husband, always was ready to face the realities of life.

"I think that working for Joe would be a fine place to start; however, you should know that there are many opportunities here just in case that one doesn't work out."

"But, Sarah, I hate to move out there without a solid future for Nate. There always seem to be opportunities out there, but he never seems to latch onto one."

"Dora, you've been away from Binghamton for so long you forgot that this is a small town;

everybody knows everybody. Your family is here. This is not the big, hard, cruel city like New York. And by the way this is truly a better place to raise your kids."

※ ※

Dora related the idea of a move to Binghamton to Nate one night after dinner. While there were unmistaken signs of worry and frustration on her face, her feelings were tempered by a positive outlook no doubt passed down to her from her parents who had worked hard and succeeded in making a new life in the harsh Binghamton environment. Dora was reaching out to her family, hoping that she and Nate would somehow find security and a new start. She thought back to their dating days and the way her family had welcomed Nate. Perhaps history would repeat itself even in the face of what she had learned about Nate's weaknesses.

Nate was silent, staring at the wall, working a toothpick in his mouth, then quickly grabbed for his handkerchief as a sneeze seemed to come at him from nowhere. This was no joking matter and his eyes seem to tear up a little.

The thought of moving his family back to Binghamton opened again the basic issues regarding his ability or desire to take on the responsibility of a family. He did not like it and furthermore wasn't too good at it.

His thoughts went back to the events of the last 15 years. How did a kid from New Jersey end up selling real estate in this little town in New York State? He never intended to put down roots there. After all, he was a guy who liked sports and the big city. One of his greatest pleasures was to spend Sunday with the *New York Times*. In Binghamton, it was difficult if not impossible to find the *Sunday Times*. He would be 200 miles away from the Brooklyn Dodgers in a city that had no major league sports at all. How did this playboy who had little interest in marriage and family end up, it seemed like almost overnight, with a wife and three children in this predicament? This little burg where men were men because they mowed the lawn in the summer, shoveled snow in the winter, repaired all the trivial things that went wrong at home, and, if they wanted to participate in sports, they would go fishing in the rivers or go hunting deer up in the mountains.

He was acutely aware that Dora was feeling insecure and panicky. He had promised her that he would do her no harm. Did he love her or was he meeting an obligation? He had not provided her with at least a minimum of financial security. Perhaps, he thought, a move back to her hometown where she could be with her mother and sisters would at least surround her with people who loved her and could provide her with basic security. It would be the right thing to do and maybe the only thing he could do.

He wasn't convinced that working for Joe's real estate company was a good idea. He would have to learn the real estate business, and he doubted that he could ever become a licensed agent. He didn't have even a basic knowledge of houses.

His thoughts turned to his children. Yes, Binghamton would be a better place to raise his children. He felt confident that his son and his new young daughter would thrive in this small-town environment.

My older sister had just graduated high school and would soon get a good job as a secretary in Manhattan. She had a boyfriend from Brooklyn, a really likable guy whom everybody liked. She was not part of this contemplated move.

"Now I wish I'd gone to college or at least gotten some training for a profession. I just didn't care at that point of my life. I only wanted a few bucks in my pocket and freedom. If only I could earn more money and give Dora all the things she wants. I would have more self-confidence to stand up to her and tell her that Binghamton was for visiting only."

What Nate failed to understand was that men of modest means may assume positions of strength and leadership through their love, behavior, personal qualities, and most importantly how they care for their family. If Nate didn't know this by this point in his life, he would certainly learn it through hard lessons in the next few years.

He knew little about Joe Goodman as a person. It was so easy to be swayed by Joe's bragging persona. Nate was troubled because he would be taking on the full responsibility of moving his family 200 miles to an unknown future relying on a new job in a new business that he did not know, counting on the leadership of his brother-in-law, whose true accomplishments were unknown. Nate apparently had not even superficially explored the facts, the figures, and the trajectory of Joe's business but rather trusted my mother who in turn had been trusting her sisters.

He was reminded of how his father had trusted a business partner and how this trust led to failure and disappointment.

Chapter 15

Our move to Binghamton in 1948 coincided with the spring or Easter break at school. Having made a couple of short trips there with my parents, I had a few vague memories of Binghamton. I remembered single-family homes with nicely trimmed lawns. Unlike Brooklyn and New York City, there were few people in the streets and very little automobile traffic. People seem relaxed, moved about slowly, and talked with a funny accent.

I knew something about small towns from the Archie Andrews comic strip. Archie had friends, albeit not all very bright, and a couple of pretty girlfriends. He was always the center of attention—sometimes getting into and then out of trouble.

My friends had a blank look on their faces when I told them I was moving to Binghamton; however, when they learned that it was going to be a small town like the one Archie Andrews lived in, their faces lit up with smiles, and I even saw some signs of envy.

The timing of the move presented some real problems for me. I was in the middle of a special school semester designed to combine the second half of the seventh year and the first half of the eighth year into one term. This had been a practice in the New York school system for many years. It was a way of advancing a relatively small group of students who had excelled academically through sixth grade. Those of us who were selected felt honored and proud. Much to my disappointment, the Binghamton school system had no such advanced class. I presented this issue to my mother, who no doubt was aware of it but did not hold it very high on her priority list.

"I don't know if my new junior high school in Binghamton will put me into the last half of the seventh grade or the first half of the eighth grade. I don't want to lose the advantage of skipping that I had here in Brooklyn."

"When we register you in Binghamton, we will explain this whole story and request that you be put into the eighth grade. Until then I don't see anything else that we can do."

The second issue was that I was just getting started with lessons for my bar mitzvah, which was coming up the following September. Where and with whom would I continue those special studies? The answer to that was again, "Wait until we get there."

The excitement of moving upstate to a totally pristine environment was clouded by the uncertainties involved in my overall education, which to a studious boy like me was quite important.

These uncertainties of mine were dwarfed by the more significant questions of what Nate would be doing to make a living. He had left a few weeks earlier to begin a job with Uncle Joe's real estate firm. He was living with my grandmother, and we would join him there at least temporarily until we could find a place to live. My grandmother lived close to the center of town in an old, poor neighborhood that was a long bike ride to my new junior high school. My older sister was graduating high school. Her plan was to work as a secretary in Manhattan and live with some friends in the city.

The move to Binghamton had been carefully planned with furniture and most of our personal belongings being shipped ahead. For travel that day, Dora had packed a few bags with lunch and things we would need immediately. With her customary courage and efficiency, she set out that morning with a two-year-old daughter, a 12-year-old son, and a few bags. For our first step, we took a taxi to the subway which took us to mid-Manhattan where we changed trains to Hudson Tube line, which went under the Hudson River to Hoboken, New Jersey, the main station for the Erie Lackawanna Railway. We boarded the train for a five-hour ride, taking us through Northwest New Jersey then north through Pennsylvania and then across the New York border to Binghamton. On the train after a couple of hours, my sister became restless. I kept her busy by reading her books to her, showing her special buildings through the window, and by giving repeated explanations of who would be waiting for us when we arrived in Binghamton. She finally fell asleep a couple of hours before our arrival.

As we pulled into the Binghamton station, it was dusk; through the window I could see an image of people who I thought might be my relatives, and then finally I found Nate walking along our car then stopping as our door opened and the chairs descended. I handed my sister over the stairs down to him as he stood at the open door down on the platform; my mother and I gathered our packages and suitcases and found our way clumsily down the steep train steps to meet the many aunts, uncles, and cousins, who were there to greet us.

My grandmother had a two-bedroom apartment in an old wood-frame, eight-family apartment house on Susquehanna Street just a few blocks from the river. She was alone as my grandfather had died about seven years earlier. Overweight, slow afoot, and with a language barrier, she relied heavily on others to get along. She spoke Yiddish to my aunts and mother and had many arguments with them, which of course I did not understand.

From the train station, we piled into three cars to my grandmother's place barely big enough to hold this crowd. I met my relatives, including a female cousin about one year older, who would become my first friend. They were all very happy to have us there. Their joy and warm welcome was a wonderful way to start my new adventure.

Chapter 16

My first week in Binghamton coincided with spring break, giving me a week to explore my unfamiliar environment. I was given a hand-me-down bicycle from my Aunt Selma's son who was about eight years older. It was a well-built Shelby bike still in good condition, and I was very happy and proud to have it, and, as I was to learn soon, I would be using it frequently to get around Binghamton, where practically everything a teenage boy did required travel either by bus or bike.

On my first day, I took my little sister out for a walk in her carriage.

"You can walk around the block with her and stop back at the Italian grocery, Gino's, and pick up an Italian bread for grandma," my mother said. "Walk over to the Christopher Columbus school, and let her walk around the playground there.

I want her to get some fresh air. She's been cooped up in this little apartment and is getting hard to handle."

The neighborhood located in the center of the city had been settled mostly by Italians about 50 years earlier. The Italian grocery featured many different versions of sausages, salami, and cheese. My grandmother liked their bread, which was a compliment to the local bakers since she had eaten bread from her own bakery for so many years.

The worst of the winter's weather was over and the trees on the surrounding hills were turning green. Typically, after a long, cold, and snowy winter, spring came along gradually as if deliberated by a celestial Weather Bureau. Uncle Joe owned an old two-family house on the west side of Binghamton. The upstairs tenants would be leaving at the end of June and we would move in. The lower floor was occupied by his oldest daughter and her four children. My junior high school and later my high school were easy bike rides from this house which was located also just a few blocks from recreation park that had a big beautiful carousel free to the public with no limits on rides. With its softball fields, tennis courts, children's area along with the carousel, the park was a fabulous gift to the residents of the city.

On my first day back to school, my mother and I met with the boys' counselor, a short, dark haired man with a long Italian name; they called him Cappy for short. He was a soft-spoken man who calmly delivered my unwelcomed news.

"I have put a request into your school board in Brooklyn for a copy of your records to learn more about your advanced class. Please be patient but for now I am putting you into the seventh-grade class."

It was the sad news I feared all along. I cried easily at age 12, and my eyes filled up with tears when I heard his decision. I protested quietly. He simply handed me my class schedule, motioned quietly to his office door, and I followed him upstairs to my social studies class, which was in progress at that time. He introduced me to the teacher, and she kindly gave me a desk and a couple of books. The class was studying the geography and history of New York State for which I had no interest. I only wanted to be put in the eighth grade where I belonged.

Unless bad weather forced me to take city buses to school using the limited amount of money my mother had given me, I rode my bike to the downtown area, through the busy traffic circle where two bridges crossed the intersection of the Chenango and Susquehanna Rivers, crossed over into the west side, and then pedaled about 15 blocks to my school, where I parked my bike in a special area in the basement.

In Brooklyn, my woodworking shop had primitive equipment and the class was easy. There was no swimming pool and physical education also presented little challenge. Things were quite different in my new school. The woodworking shop was new and fully equipped to instruct even advanced woodworking students. The others in my class had already learned how to use carpentry equipment; the teacher gave me some special instruction, but there was a lot for me to learn in a brief period.

The school had a beautiful swimming pool; most of the kids knew how to swim. There were rules to follow for entering the pool. We were required to scrub clean in the shower before going into the water. Older kids were there to rub our arms to make sure that our skin was dirt-free. The water was cold, and we swam in the raw. My experience in swimming was limited to the ocean in Coney Island where we splashed around and never actually learned how to swim.

The academic work was not a problem, and I was able to catch up to the class quickly, but in general I felt lost and alone and a little exhausted from the long bike ride. I did not complain to my parents because I sensed that my mother's adjustment to living with my grandmother, to taking care of a small child, and to my father's responsibility to be successful in a new job all had a much higher priority than my troubles at school.

It took a few weeks for me to become adjusted to my new school. One morning Cappy appeared in the front of my homeroom class and quietly told me to pick up my books and my jacket. I followed him out of the room. He had an eighth-grade class schedule for me. I followed him to my new homeroom. He wished me success and made me promise to contact him if I had any problems. I did not ask why or how it happened. I was simply thankful that I was finally getting what I wanted.

While my grades were only slightly better than passable during my first two terms, I became an A student. All the things that were initially so challenging and even intimidating soon became easy. I was smiling, making friends, and was friendly with the teachers. Cappy, who oversaw the school guards, invited me to join his group and, in my last term, I was made captain.

Looking back at my junior high school days, I see that Cappy clearly was a man dedicated to his job of caring for the boys in school. He had watched me quietly in his own way grow and become successful.

Chapter 17

During our first week in Binghamton, my mother called the religious schools to find out how I might pick up again with my bar mitzvah lessons. To her disappointment, all such classes were already filled and private one-on-one instruction would be far more expensive than we could afford.

We learned from my aunts that Rabbi Margolis, the religious leader of the Orthodox synagogue, had a new assistant as he was close to retirement and might have some time available. Margolis, in fact, was not an ordained rabbi, but he had the title to the congregation and had assumed all the appropriate duties including circumcision. As a cantor he had a strong, well-trained voice and was appreciated by his congregation.

Margolis remembered my mother from the time she was a young lady. He would be happy to prepare me for bar mitzvah in the Orthodox synagogue. So every other day I met with him on his porch on the south side of Binghamton and learned to chant my part by listening to him. I apparently had a good ear for music, and he was pleased with my progress.

I had learned from my parents that Margolis was the man who had circumcised me having been born in Binghamton City Hospital. It was only six months later when my father lost his job due to a cutback at the haberdashery chain and we moved to Brooklyn. What a surprise this was! The man who had circumcised me was preparing me for my bar mitzvah 13 years later. I did not broach the subject with him as I had heard from my parents that he had bragged back then of what a terrific job he had done on me.

For my bar mitzvah lessons, I rode my bike to the bridge crossing the Susquehanna River and then on to the rabbi's house on the south side. The weather was warm and breezy, and I enjoyed the ride on my new Shelby bike.

Chapter 18

Nate started working for the Joe Goodman Real Estate Agency about a month before the rest of the family moved to Binghamton. His job was to go door-to-door and identify those homes with an interest in either buying or selling. He was given neighborhoods with lower-priced homes since that was Goodman's specialty and strength. He would create a listing of homes to be followed up by a licensed real estate agent, mainly Joe Goodman. Under his arrangement with Joe, when a house that he listed was involved in a final transaction, he would be paid a fair share of the commission.

Walking from house to house, climbing stairs, and introducing himself to the owners was tedious, tiring, and sometimes frustrating work, but Nate had strong legs and could walk for hours without fatigue, which he attributed to his athletic youth.

He could look forward to a good dinner with my grandmother in the evenings. He got along with her and tolerated her old-world ideas and poor English. She reminded him of his own grandmother, who had a significant role in raising him and his three sisters, as his parents were so deeply involved day and night with their businesses. He chuckled when he recalled how she mispronounced the word "teeth." At bedtime she would admonish the children, "Don't forget to brush the tits; brush the tits." He would laugh, teasing his sisters, imitating her, shaking his finger at the girls. "Did you brush your tits tonight?"

The job entailed walking for hours in the cold, damp Binghamton weather, but he reminded himself that winter was ending, and he could look forward to a pleasant spring.

One day, after being outdoors for a few hours, he decided to drop into a luncheonette for some coffee to warm himself. The chilly air had exhilarated him, and his growing list of potential homes made him feel confident in the future as he thought to himself, "Yeah, sure enough this is a gamble bringing my family out here on a job that I've never done before. I've got about 75 names listed. All I need is for one or two to pay off."

The good news was that Binghamton was growing at a fast pace. The postwar era was bringing photographic manufacturing, including camera and film from captured German companies. In addition, IBM had a great future, because all the new communication technologies developed for the Army and Navy would soon become consumer products. Nate thought to himself, "I have a good chance of listing a couple of winners per month, which would bring me at least $1000 and maybe even $2000."

It was with this optimism that he met his arriving family at the train station that night. He was proud of his family. His children were smart and good-looking. His son stood over six feet tall, which amazed everybody. His little two-year-old daughter, Ruth Ann, had blond, curly hair and a smile for everybody. The cousins vied over a chance to hold her, saying, "She is beautiful! Can I hold her now? Please give her to me."

Uncle Joe was there, black hair slightly oiled, combed straight back above wire-rimmed glasses and the ever-present cigar. Joe was genuinely pleased to see us and welcomed us as if he were a member of the Chamber of Commerce. He was playing a critical role in our lives not only because he was providing our livelihood but also because in just a couple months we would be moving into one of his houses on the preferred west side of Binghamton. There was so much to learn about Joe Goodman; the real man would occasionally peep out from under his self-assured persona.

We piled into four cars and filled my grandmother's house wall to wall. Most of the excitement and talk was about my little sister.

Later I would be asked if I resented how much more attention she received. After all, not too long ago, I was the baby of the family. In fact, in later years, a psychiatrist asked the same question. "I may be suppressing it, but I have no memory of such a feeling," I replied. "I was aware of her magnetism. I can understand the attention she attracted."

Chapter 19

Our new home on the west side of Binghamton was probably the oldest house on Rotary Avenue although the location was close to Recreation Park, West Junior High school, and buses going downtown. My cousin Hannah, her husband Henry, and their four small children lived in the downstairs apartment. Hannah's kids were loud and noisy and frequently misbehaved. Fortunately, we had a large backyard which helped contain their energies. Her children were also active at night as all four wet their beds. In the morning the heavy odor of urine floated through the entire building. There were times when the fumes from the kids combined with the smell of frying bacon was more than Dora could endure.

There was no central heat in this old building. We brought a coal stove into the living room and one into the kitchen which also served as a cooking range. My mother had learned how to operate coal stoves in her childhood. I eventually learned how to add coal to the fire, help her carry ashes out to our back porch, and then eventually tote them downstairs to be taken away. The evenings were warm enough, but the fire usually went out in the middle of a frosty winter night, so I dressed for school in frigid conditions.

The walls **were** in miserable shape and depressing to look at. Dora immediately went into action purchasing attractive wallpapers and learning from the shopkeeper the art and science of papering a wall. Working on her ironing board, she learned the proper way of folding and applying the glue and hanging paper in sections on the wall. She discovered how to make straight borders and how to match the pattern uniformly from piece to piece. Remarkably, in about a week's time, we had professionally papered walls. My relatives marveled at how she had transformed that apartment from a dump into a reasonably lovely place to live. They knew or were reminded how resourceful my mother could be. While I was proud of her achievement, I was beginning to get accustomed to the way she could conquer just about every challenge.

When the weather got warm, the walls in my bedroom became covered with dead mosquitoes as I was up in the night swatting them. The stairs to the attic led from my bedroom and a quick walk-through revealed an open irreparable window. Dora and I covered those openings with plastic film, so that I was no longer covered by mosquito bites and could sleep peacefully again.

That summer I made friends with the boy in the next house. We rode our bikes together and I saw most of the city's west side. Larry was an avid stamp collector, and I eventually caught the bug from him. We biked to the stamp dealer who lived in a small apartment on the street directly above the Chenango River. With frequent visits, our stamp collections expanded as we spent whatever little money each of us could collect.

As the school semester started, we each got busy with our classes. He was a few grades lower, so for the most part we went our separate ways until Christmastime when Larry received a unique gift from his parents that would have a profound effect on my life.

Chapter 20

I was a young newcomer, age 12, to a strange city, and my relatives offered suggestions on how and where to find friends my age. Aunt Sarah saw this as a wonderful opportunity for her youngest daughter Ellen to reach out to me. Although several years older, she invited me to their house to perhaps become friends. Ellen was built short and stocky like her father, and I thought that she walked like him as well. Unfortunately, she inherited his large nose. (As Nate would say, "Do long noses run in your family?") Five or six years later she would have her nose reconstructed and I thought it was an improvement, but somehow her new nose didn't go along with the rest of her face.

Ellen and I spent many fun hours riding our bikes around Recreation Park, stopping for ice cream and popcorn and for a few rides on the park's great carousel that was free with unlimited rides to one and all. She talked about the teachers, classes, and activities at the junior high school. In general, she gave me a lot of guidance about the city, places to go, and how to travel. I appreciated her friendship and the time spent in Sarah's nicely decorated house. We spent many hours in their den playing Monopoly. Usually it was just the two of us as Ellen's two older sisters had married and moved to Florida, and my aunt was often shopping or visiting her many friends.

One afternoon Ellen got up and left our game to go to the bathroom. After waiting for what seemed like an unusually long time, I got up and looked down the hallway which led to several bedrooms and bathroom. At the end of the hall in the last bedroom there was, sideways to the door, a large dressing table with a mirror. Ellen was standing there without blouse and bra looking into the mirror intently observing herself. I was at an age of great sexual curiosity and just beginning to learn but not having seen examples of the differences between men and women. Her breasts appeared to be full and curvaceous and seemed to thrust forward as if anticipating some future encounter. About five seconds passed when she looked down the hallway and saw me standing there and quickly closed the door.

Back at the Monopoly table, she looked carefully into my face, smiled and asked, "What did you just see? How much did you see?"

"I didn't see anything. I just was looking for you because you'd been away for a while."

"Are you sure you didn't see anything? Are you sure you didn't see me?"

"No, Ellen, I didn't see anything." Of course, I was lying. I was obviously uncomfortable, and she knew it.

We went back to our game and it was never mentioned. I have often wondered how the conversation would have gone had I said, "Yes, Ellen, I did see you staring into the mirror admiring your tits. I have never seen bare tits before. Yours look very big and nice."

What would she have said then?

Chapter 21

My next-door neighbor Larry invited me to his home to see his Christmas tree and all the decorations of the season. He was quite excited about his presents under the tree. Boxes and wrapping paper were strewn over the living room floor. This was the time of the year when I thought Christian children were so lucky. I took advantage of my invitation and walked around and looked at everything. It was my first Christmas morning at a Christian home. His house smelled good, maybe from cookies or something else sweet. I envied how Christmas had brought so much goodness to Larry's home.

I held back my emotions until my eye caught a funny-shaped plastic thing identified on the package as an ocarina. It was a toy musical instrument with a series of four or five numbered holes. By covering selected openings, one could blow into this thing and create musical notes. It was accompanied by a small song book with numbers corresponding to popular Christmas songs. The thought of making music really intrigued me, and I couldn't put it down. Larry was much more interested in some of the model cars and trains he had received. I wanted the little ocarina and I offered to trade him, but he showed little interest; however, the following day I brought up the subject again and offered my entire stamp collection, for which I had lost interest, in return for the toy ocarina.

After Larry accepted the trade, I brought the ocarina with me to Sunday School, thinking I would show it off to some of my classmates after class, but that plan was suddenly interrupted. A few of the boys were in a big hurry heading downstairs towards the basement. One of them whispered to me on the way down, "Stan Summers has some dirty pictures!"

Stan Summers was a straight A student; remarkably at age 13 he was one of the best clarinet players in the city. He had a reputation for sleeping only about four hours every night, because he was so busy playing in various groups in the area. Stan was the only child of a divorced mother who doted on him and showed a tremendous interest in his education and cultural development. As far as we knew, he had no contact with his father and never talked about him.

Among his many and varied interests Stan had a fascination for what we used to call "dirty pictures." He had enough money and knew the right people to buy pornographic pictures, which on rare occasions he would share with us. These were amateur photographs—blurry pictures on inferior quality paper. Nevertheless, most of us were thrilled to get some new insights into what was for us pure sexual fantasy. So even though the pictures were of inferior quality, we were happy to get a glimpse of real sex. Stan was our leader in sexual education.

Under a light in the basement, we huddled around Stan as he held a picture in his hand close to his chest. This was a picture of a nude man and woman having intercourse, but their position confused this sexually unenlightened group of young boys.

"It looks like she's on top of him."

"Yeah, but she's facing up and I can see his face under her head is facing up also."

"This is a rip off; you can't do it that way."

"How do you know so much? How many times have you done it?

Finally, Stan replied to this speculation and confusion. "For sure, I know this is real; can't you see his dick coming up right there?" he said pointing. We leaned closer to the picture to see what he meant, but at that moment he quickly added, "I got to put this away; if I get caught with this, I'm in deep trouble."

So the session ended, and we ran up the stairs slightly better informed although that picture raised more questions than it answered.

Although it was anti-climactic, I took out the ocarina and started to play a Christmas carol from the little book that came with it. Stan was the only one who showed an interest in my musical performance and walked over to me.

"If you want to play a musical instrument, why don't you play the clarinet like I do?"

"How many years have you been playing the clarinet, Stan?"

"I started about four or five years ago. I have an extra clarinet; it's the one I started on, and I could loan it to you. I have a lesson Tuesday night after school. You should come join us. My teacher will show you the basics of how to play and he won't charge anything. If you like it, you can keep my clarinet until you get a better one."

Stan had an expensive professional Selmer clarinet, and, after years with the area's best teacher and many hours of practice, he had become an outstanding clarinet player.

After a few lessons and little help from Stan, I became good enough to join the Junior High School Band.

My progress was hampered by the fact that I played most notes extremely flat. My teacher and the bandleader Mr. Lynch finally became a little annoyed and frustrated by the fact that there was no improvement in my tone. Stan himself was equally dismayed, and finally one day he took a good hard look at his horn.

"You know this mouthpiece is only made from plastic. It's very old and it looks like it has lost its shape. I really think you should go over to the music store downtown and buy yourself a new mouthpiece."

On the very next Saturday morning, I rode my bike downtown to our biggest department store, went up to the music department, and paid six dollars for a new mouthpiece. The change in my tone was dramatic—so much so that Mr. Lynch interrupted our next band practice to ask me what I had done differently.

"It's just a new mouthpiece, Mr. Lynch."

He smiled happily, and I was on my way to becoming a good clarinet player but only a distant second to Stan.

A couple of years later Stan's mother married a wealthy man from Boston. They moved away. Stan went to prep school in New England and finally to Harvard and Harvard Medical School.

By default, I became the first chair clarinet player in the high school band.

Chapter 22

One evening during our first August in Binghamton, this after-dinner conversation between Dora and Nate was overheard:

"On top of all the household bills, we have a bar mitzvah coming up in just a few weeks with many new expenses including a payment to the rabbi."

"I know, I know; don't worry we'll find the money."

"You've been working for Joe now for about six months, and I haven't seen a single dollar in commission come through yet."

"Well, it's not because I haven't been listing houses."

"Well, do you know how many actual houses you have listed?"

Nate

"Yes, I do because there's a book in Joe's office where I file all leads, and I know that the number is 53."

"Do you mean to say that you've listed 53 houses and none of them sold? What the hell is going on here?"

"I've been wondering that myself. I'm going to do some investigating."

There were other things in general that were bothering Nate about Joe's business. There seemed to be a lack of activities in the office that usually typify a robust business. Nate decided to investigate Joe's business to get some answers.

He had often heard the name Gillies mentioned by the office secretary to people who desperately needed to contact Joe. Sometimes when his signature on a closing document or contract was needed, the secretary would say something that sounded like, "He can be found at Gillie's."

Having lived and worked in Binghamton about 15 years ago as a single guy, Nate had heard of Gillie's but had never been there. He looked up the address in the phone book. Gillie's could be found on a side street running from Court Street.

Binghamton was the county seat of Broome County, and the marble pillared courthouse was situated at the center of town. Running north of the courthouse was Chenango Street and running west was Court Street. Intersecting at the small park in front of the courthouse, these two streets made up the major business district of the city. Buses from all points of the city had stops near the courthouse. On Thursday and Saturday nights, the business district was well lit with shoppers lining the sidewalks and filling the stores in evidence of postwar prosperity.

It was about 1:00 on a Wednesday afternoon when Nate opened the front door to Gillie's and found himself in a small storefront with magazine racks and various tobacco products in a glass showcase. As he entered there was no one in the room. Opposite the front entrance was a door leading to a much larger room. He quickly found four card tables with brightly lit by lamps suspended above the playing surface. The tables were empty except for dishes and glasses apparently left after lunch with remnants like partially eaten bread crusts, left over salad, and empty Coke and ginger ale bottles. Ashtrays were filled with cigarette butts and partially-smoked cigars. Remaining wisps of tobacco smoke could be seen under the lights. The opposite end of the room was dark except for a bright lamp that hung over each of two pool tables. These tables were so well lit that they reminded Nate of a night baseball game at Yankee Stadium. He could see about four or five men moving about the tables talking quietly and laughing. Their movements created odd-shaped shadows under the bright lamps.

Joe Goodman was concentrating intently on his next shot as he walked confidently up to one of the tables, chalking a cue stick in his right hand. His steps were more deliberate than usual, and he seemed to dig his heels into the floor slightly. He leaned over the table calling the shot he was attempting, voice muffled through one side of his mouth as he clung tightly to a cigar in the other. The sound of a pool ball falling into the pocket broke the silence, and he slowly straightened himself with a smile of success as others congratulated him on what appeared to be a challenging shot.

※ ※

Nate made several more trips to Gillies's during the next two weeks, staying just long enough to convince himself that Joe Goodman was there and involved.

On one occasion Joe was seated at the card table when he noticed Nate.

"Hi, brother-in-law; come on in have a seat. Want to join us for a little gin rummy?"

Nate shook his head and said, "No, thanks. I got to get back to work."

Later that night he reported back to my mother. "Yeah, that's where he's spending his time. I figure he's probably either playing cards or shooting pool about 80 and 90% of the working week, and that's why he's not selling houses."

Dora replied, "But how is he earning enough money at least for his own family?"

"I believe he's selling just enough each month—just enough to give Anna money to run the house."

"Maybe that's why Anna rarely goes out or rarely spends any money."

Dora became angry and tears filled her eyes as she thought about how her sister could bring her here to work for Joe knowing that his real estate business was a sham. Why, she asked herself, does this man have such bad luck with jobs? She added this question to the one on her luck with men.

Chapter 23

That night she was kept awake by thoughts of the many jobs Nate had attempted and lost. Her sisters had talked her into coming to Binghamton. Were they naïve; were they sincere? She had so many questions that she didn't know where to start. Getting a good night's sleep would be helpful. Her anger was somewhat tempered by the fact that Binghamton was her hometown, and she was more comfortable here than in New York City, especially since it was probably a better place to raise children. She had grown up here and knew that it was good for children. It wasn't until the wee hours of the morning that she dozed off to sleep, having comforted herself with the thought of talking to Sarah tomorrow. Sarah was an older sister whom she trusted for good judgment. She would know more about Joe Goodman. She would get the full story from Sarah. Yes, Sarah was never one to skimp when it comes to articulating the full story.

"Sarah, it's been about six months now. Nate has worked hard and has gotten what he says is about 50 leads. But none of Nate's houses have sold."

"Dora, in a way I'm not surprised to hear this. I must tell you that for the last couple of years Anna has kept a very tight budget. I don't think she's had a new dress in a long time, and the car they drive is not what you'd expect from a man who owns a real estate agency. She doesn't talk very much about Joe's business. In fact, I've been suspicious that she's so silent about it. Anyway, this doesn't help your situation, and it doesn't help Nate find a job where he can make a decent living."

"What has become so shocking to me, and I'm not sure that Anna knows about this, so I want you to promise to keep what I'm going to tell you a strict secret—Nate discovered that Joe is spending a lot of his time at Gillie's. I'm not sure how accurate this is, but it appears that he spends his mornings playing cards and afternoons shooting pool. This kind of thing can be addictive. I wonder if he's addicted?"

"Dora, I have been living with such conflict ever since you decided to move to Binghamton. On the one hand, I wanted to tell you about Joe and his gambling addiction, but on the other hand Anna made me swear that I would keep it secret. So now it's not a secret anymore. Please don't be upset about being here in Binghamton without a job for Nate; just remember we are your family, and we'll always take care of you."

Dora, sobbing, barely able to get words out, said, "You just don't know what I've been going through all these years. I don't mind sacrificing; I don't need a lot of clothes. I don't need housekeeping help. I don't need a lot of special entertainment. I just want to feel secure. I just want to know how much money we're getting each week, big or small; I just want to have confidence."

Sarah paused for a while trying to take on a calming tone of voice. Sarah was a person totally overwhelmed by the people and events in her life. She was so taken by her own life, she would talk fast and endlessly, attempting to bring others up to date on the events of her life. But when it came to empathizing with her own blood, Sarah could be warm and loving.

"I want to tell you something about Isaac's business although maybe it's not the right time, but he has plans to expand the store. There's a lot of space in the back for additional shelves and maybe even a new counter. In the front of the store, he occasionally puts boxes of food out for people to pick and touch, but there is plenty of room for quite a few more out there. The expansion would represent a significant boost in sales. To do this expansion, he needs another person in the store who can watch the present business, make sure people get what they need, and make certain there is no stealing. In other words, he needs somebody who knows the business—somebody he can trust. Now if that person is Nate, I'm sure that Isaac would be glad to bring him in. The pay is not great, but it would be a reasonably good living for your family. And while working for Isaac, Nate could keep his eye out for something better. I would never tell that to Isaac, but it's a fact."

After hanging up the phone, Dora thought to herself, "What a combination of men—a tall, thin city boy and a short muscular country boy. I doubt if they would have more than 10 words to say to each other; they really have nothing in common. In fact, Nate likes to joke about Isaac being a farm boy with short legs. 'Have you heard that Isaac is going to sue the city? Yeah, he claims that they built the sidewalk too close to his ass.'"

Chapter 24

No one expected Nate and Sam to get along well. They were about as different as one could imagine. Sam was strong and muscular and could easily lift heavy boxes of produce, whereas Nate was wiry, flexible, and agile and could move quickly—probably from his athletic youth. Sam was direct and blunt in his dealings with people while Nate was a true salesman, always had a smile, and was considerate of everyone's feelings. Sam had grown up with long hours doing hard, strenuous farm work. Demanding work for Nate was pounding the pavements of New York going door-to-door and calling on his clients. The one difference that bothered Nate the most was the way Sam talked. The combination of his heavy upstate New York accent along with the high pitch of his voice made sounds so strange that all Nate could think of was a dumb farmer who had never been off the farm.

"Nate, I got three crates of cabbages in the back. Bring them up front where people can see them as soon as they walk in and put a price sign over them."

"Nate, those big juice and soup cans are too damn high; I want them down lower where people can reach them. Take this ladder and go up there and hand them down to me one at a time, and I'll stack them on this here shelf."

So, it was "Nate pick that up; Nate move that box; Nate carry this; Nate carry that." After a few days Nate ended up in bed with agonizing back pains. He could hardly move. Sitting up to eat was a painful effort.

A few days later Nate responded to an ad in the *Binghamton Press* for a door-to-door salesman with the American Furniture and Jewelry Company. This was a locally-owned company that featured small furniture items like telephone tables, small appliances like toasters, living room lamps, religious pictures framed, and jewelry such as low-priced watches and jewelry boxes. The actual inventory varied depending on whether the owner could find big lots or odd lots at greatly reduced prices. The salesman would load their cars with demonstration samples of hot items and merchandise the boss wanted to push. The county was divided up into five or six sales territories comprising the poorest neighborhoods. Customers were shown attractive luxuries they never dreamed of owning but could have for a dollar or two down and $.50 to a dollar collected per week. Customers were usually not aware that they were paying two or three times the retail price.

Owner and President of the American Furniture and Jewelry Company Gabby Friedlander was a friendly, easy-going, medium-sized man with dark wavy hair and horn-rimmed glasses. He made direct eye contact which, along with his big smile, helped make him an outstanding salesman. Gabby walked and moved around quickly yet silently on thick crepe foam shoes.

"Come on in, Nate; have a seat. I've been expecting you. Can we get you something to drink?"

"No, thanks. I been drinking coffee out in your office area and talking to some of your people."

"Based on everything I've heard about you Nate, I think you're the kind of person we're looking for. You would be our fourth salesman. We've got a territory laid out and ready. The reason I say that is that, like the saying goes, we sell the sizzle more than the steak. We treat our customers with a smile; we put them at ease with no pressure.

The way it works is that we simply bring to their house one or two items that we carry. Like a kid in a toy store, they start wishing they could have it but can't afford it. We come to the rescue. You'll find that if you tell them that you can give them a discount, this week only, they love it and they will buy the item."

Now our guys work hard to be honest, but they make a good living between commission and salary. Talk to them and you'll hear it from them."

"Oh, for sure, Gabby. I can do this job, and I would like to start as soon as possible. Also, is there any way that I can get an advance? The move and everything has really drained us."

"Sure, Nate. I can give you a $50 advance, and I'll tell the girls to work it off the books slowly."

At home that night, Nate was happy to break the news to Dora about his new job.

"Yeah, no problem. I know I can do this and I can bring my salary up to maybe even $10,000 a year; of course, not right away."

After they both considered all the positive aspects and the possible bright future that this job might bring, they started to face one big fat reality:

the job required a car which they did not have; even worse, Nate did not have a driver's license.

So he started the job with my mother driving. She got her license years earlier as a single girl and now only had to renew it. She needed a place to leave my little sister. Downstairs with Hannah and the four bedwetters was a simple, logical solution needed only until Nate would get his own driver's license.

Nate failed the driver's test seven times, and this put a heavy burden on Dora and the rest of the family who needed to pitch in and take on some of her responsibilities as she was driving the car.

Chapter 25

Money was tight during those first few years in Binghamton. Entering high school my own needs were growing, and I was reluctant to ask my mother for money. Part time jobs were quite rare. Having the right contacts, teenagers from established families sometimes found part-time or summer jobs.

We need a break here," I thought. "Someone in my family needs to break this run of bad luck." As far back as I could remember we never had enough money. My mother would always carefully budget every dollar she had. I always had the impression, and it probably came from her, that my father was not earning as much as other men. His relatives would support him by arguing with my mother that she spent too much on food and clothing and that these were areas where she could economize. Dora wanted us to be well fed and to look as good as possible.

Nate

As if a prayer was answered, I was given a chance to earn my own money in the newspaper business. Although it was only about $12 a week, it was enough to make me independent.

The city had two newspapers, *The Press* and *The Sun*, and these seemed to meet needs during the week; however; the Sunday papers from cities like New York and Philadelphia offered many special sections from fashion to comics to major reviews of the news by prominent writers.

Sunday papers from New York and Philadelphia were available in a limited number of retail stores that were open on Sunday mornings. The Pearson News Company brought these papers in by train or air and delivered them late Saturday night or early Sunday morning to those places that were open as a service to the few willing to get up early Sunday morning and drive for a paper.

My friend Ronny Klein and his brother Donny had acquired 2 sets of wheels from a discarded baby carriage, and with limited tools had attached a couple of orange crates. With support from their parents, they had convinced Pearson to deliver papers in heavy, wire-wrapped packages to be delivered to about 150 homes in the neighborhood. It was a good business. The boys paid $0.19 for a *Sunday New York Times,* which they sold for $ 0.25.

About a year later brother Donny lost interest in the papers when he got a permanent job. My friend Ronny asked me to take his brother's place. We would begin early Sunday morning cutting the wire on the heavy packages of paper and loading them into the wagon. We pushed the wagon up and down hills and delivered papers according to a list of names and addresses they had accumulated. Customers paid for the paper by leaving the exact change on their doorstep. Around noon we finished our deliveries, took a bus to the Pearson warehouse, paid for our papers, and then split the profits.

A few months later Ronnie's parents decided that he could handle the deliveries himself and take all the profit; after all, Ronny and his brother had started the business. Then I was broke again but not without hope.

Dora remembered Manny Pearson from her high school days. In fact, he courted her and probably wanted to marry her. She recalled politely turning him down saying that she was not ready to get serious. As she remembered, he was too short and not very good-looking.

She telephoned him and said, "Hello, Manny, this is Dora. I hope you remember me. How have you been all these years?"

"Hello, Dora. I heard that you and your family had moved back to Binghamton. Welcome back."

She got up enough courage to ask him for a big favor.

"Manny, my son has been delivering Sunday papers with Ronnie Klein. Now Ronnie wants to handle the entire route himself. I'm wondering if you happen to know if my neighborhood is getting delivery of Sunday papers. Let's say starting with Rotary Avenue then going for five blocks west, south, and even north from here."

"Yes, I know exactly what you are talking about, Dora, and, no, they are not getting a paper, and it would be a fine opportunity for your son. I'm happy to help you. Let me tell you how to get started. Mimeograph a stack of notices with an offer to deliver any of the New York or Philadelphia Sunday papers on their doorstep and simply give your phone number. Have your son put one in all the mailboxes in your area. Then simply sit by the phone and the orders will come in. I can promise you."

"When we have enough customers to start a paper route, how can we get you to start delivery of the papers?"

"That part is easy, Dora," he replied. "Simply give me a call and tell me the quantities you need, and the packages will be delivered at your door about 6 a.m. the next Sunday morning."

My Sunday morning paper business was an important turning point in my life. It gave me enough money to be independent and in a sense added to the family income. The great difficulties my father had in trying to secure a permanent job and our shortage of money had weighed heavily on me emotionally. Now, with a few bucks in my pocket, I was able to accept my situation and saw my father through the eyes of a loving son. I never stopped laughing at his jokes, and I was still overjoyed when he came home at night.

Nate seemed proud of me as he drove me to Pearson to pay my bill on Sunday afternoon after deliveries.

"Well, Charlie, how much did you clear this week?" he asked with a smile as he picked up his free copy of the *Sunday New York Times*, compliments of my paper business. (He always called me Charlie; no one could figure why, but then he called his mother Jo, which he explained was short for Josephine; in fact, her name was Bertha.)

Chapter 26

After two years with American Furniture and Jewelry, Nate was finally secure. He was well-liked and accepted by his customers thanks to his sales and solid record of weekly collections. He was making a good living and could afford a wide-screen TV and some nice clothes for his little girl Ruth Ann. We had a new car, although one couldn't call it a family car because the backseat was loaded with sales samples. Unfortunately, the monthly payments on the car took a sizable chunk of Nate's earnings. Dora lamented at the end of the month that he was working for the car.

I was a high school student. I played clarinet in the band and orchestra and studied college prep courses. I had a full schedule but nevertheless maintained an awareness of what was going on in Nate's life. His job was demanding because Binghamton winters were snowy and cold; the midsummers were hot and humid. He came home exhausted and caught a bad cold every winter. His biggest pleasures came from sports on TV. In addition to the usual football and baseball, there was boxing from Madison Square Garden every Friday night. He enjoyed watching bloody-faced fighters dance around and sock each other into oblivion.

Social life for a teenage boy in Binghamton required a car, especially if you had a hot date and wanted some privacy. Some of my friends were able to use their father's car, and I went on double dates with them. There were times, though, that I had a date with a special girl and wanted to be out alone with her. I tried to borrow our car, knowing that it was meant for business and that the backseat was loaded with merchandise.

"Dad, I've got a date tonight, and I'm going to wear my new suit to the school dance."

"That's nice. Who's the girl?"

"Do you think I could borrow your car tonight instead of using buses and cabs?"

"No, no, the backseat is loaded with stuff, and you'll be tempting every bum on the street to steal."

"I'll take everything out of the car and put it in the hallway," I assured him. Reluctantly he handed the key over to me.

I thought I had removed everything from the car, but that wasn't quite right. I parked that night at my date's house, walked around, and opened her door. As she started to get out, she accidentally bumped into the visor and knocked a small photograph down onto the floor face up. It was a picture of a naked fat lady facing the camera and squatting. It was not sexy but rather grotesque and ridiculous. We laughed mostly out of embarrassment. In defense, I explained that my father was quite a comedian and that this picture was strictly for laughs.

※

A friend at school worked as a stock boy in my father's company. One day he said to me, "Your father is the funniest guy I have ever met."

I smiled and responded "Yeah, we think he's funny too. Has he been doing some crazy things at work?"

"The salesman all come into the office early in the morning before they go out on their routes. They kid around a lot with the ladies. They tell some funny stories over a cup of coffee. But your father is a standout among them. He's hilarious and people fall off their chairs laughing at him. He came in one day last week with a handful of condoms and went around blowing them up and throwing them at the ladies and asking if they'd buy one or two for $1.50 a week. He would tell them that if their house doesn't have any condoms, they should put a few on their coffee table."

That night I tried to visualize the scene. I pictured a frosty winter morning with people arriving at the office which was just beginning to warm up. Lights turning on, secretaries uncovering their typewriters, everyone resentful of having to leave their warm beds. Everyone trying to face the day and trying to get themselves started. In comes Nate saying "hello" to everybody and trying to wake people up, joking around with the ladies, especially the good-looking ones, and then asking if people had enough condoms. If not, he says he has a big supply; then he starts to blow them up and throws them around like balloons. I know from experience that his antics to most people would seem silly and even stupid. But when he did this kind of stuff, it was hilarious and people couldn't stop laughing.

And then, as I pictured it, everybody would begin the day's work. The salesman would head out for their cars, Gabby would head back to his office, stock boys would return to the warehouse, and the secretaries would return to their desks and quietly remove the covers from their typewriters. A typical, routine day was about to start, and yet. there was a difference, maybe a small one, but I could detect a change on their faces—a little smile that persisted as a remnant of the morning's laughter.

That night I fantasized that I was lecturing an audience of sophisticated and learned people. My topic was the hilarious behavior of Nate Rubin to be explained or justified. I tried to approach his humor from as many aspects as I could. One theory I presented was that the world was entirely too serious.

"The world is getting entirely too serious," I said as I tried to look at everybody right in the eyes. "Have you noticed how serious people are? How they lost all perspective? How they can't see the funny side of life?

"It's been proven that laughter reduces blood pressure, and it has been proven that humor reduces stress and anxiety, and you know how much of that we have. It's understandable. First the enormous task of building up our military strength to win World War II. Now we worry about the Soviet Union and we live with the fear of nuclear obliteration. Of course, we're serious but there are some people—and I don't know if it's in their blood or where they got it—there are some people who still see the funny side of things and feel that comedy is a pleasant way to socially interact with one another."

Chapter 27

Aunt Sarah was a warm, big-hearted although somewhat naïve lady. Slightly overweight, her feet were noticeably long and narrow. (I called her Aunt Long- shoes. People laughed and said that I would grow up to be a funny man like my father.) She was proud of her hard-working husband and three daughters and always had a lot to say about every incident in their lives. (I knew one that she didn't—her youngest admiring her boobs in the mirror.) In fact, Sarah talked endlessly with passion, jumping quickly from one subject to another. She rarely slowed down to let her listener get a word in edgewise.

Dora was a good listener by nature and made an easy target for Sarah to unload her storehouse of stories and pent-up feelings. I would see Dora sitting at the dining room table listening to Sarah on the telephone for hours. I knew it was Sarah on the other end because my mother was simply holding the phone up, switching ears every five minutes, saying nothing, just listening.

Her conversation was the same on her visits to our house except that the rest of us could hear these incredible monologues. One late afternoon my mother was standing in the kitchen preparing our dinner, and Sarah was sitting at the table talking. Dora was tired and short on patience that afternoon and as a result allowed herself to interject her opinion about the subject of the day using words and a tone clearly critical of Sarah.

Taken aback, Sarah opened her eyes wide, took a deep, noisy breath, and fired back, "You know, Dora, you are a person who assumes a superior attitude to others. You actually enjoy finding weaknesses or faults in others." She paused and relaxed a little. "Well, of course, everybody does this to some extent." Then forcefully, angrily shaking her head, she continued, "But most of us file such observations somewhere tucked away in our minds. In your case, though, you go right for the jugular (motioning toward her throat) and expose someone's weaknesses."

At this point Dora completely lost her patience and willpower and boldly fired back at her older sister. "You know, Sarah, why don't you *kish mir in tuches* (kiss my ass)?"

Flustered and highly insulted, Sarah rose from the table and made a beeline for the door. She wasn't seen again for many months. In fact, my mother commented to Nate one evening, "You may not have noticed it, but several months have gone by and I haven't talked to Sarah. And what do you know, I've been a lot more relaxed, and I seem to have more time to do the things I need to do."

Nate was silent. He had nothing against Sarah, but for him this was another example of how his family including his English-speaking mother rose above his Binghamton in-laws. His comparison quickly went to his sister Ruth who, along with her husband, had been a staunch Zionist and had worked with some of the most influential people in this country, including Golda Meir, toward the realization of a homeland for the Jewish people. Efforts such as these finally led to the creation of the state of Israel. This kind of comparative thinking acted like a soothing balm to his ego which, over the years and now under Dora's family control, had been severely battered.

The hiatus between my mother and Aunt Sarah ended a few months later quite literally by accident.

Aunt Sarah's house was about midway down a steep street leading down from my junior high school. Biking my way home, I would fly down that street turning left at the bottom. One day sand had accumulated at the corner causing my bike to skid onto its side with my head scraping the road putting a gash above my left eye. My face was quickly covered in blood. Although my house was just two blocks away, my mother would not be back home for another couple of hours, so I wrapped my bleeding forehead with my handkerchief and showed up at Aunt Sarah's back door.

"Oh my God, what happened to you," she cried out.

"I fell with my bike on the corner," I replied.

She quickly began to clean my face and stop the bleeding and then dressed the gash on my forehead while exclaiming that she "had three daughters, never had a son, so this was new to her." Nevertheless, she was caring and quite effectively nursed my wound.

She drove me home a couple of hours later and repeated a few times to my mother how shocking it was to be presented with such a situation as she had never experienced anything like this having had only daughters. My mother was so pleased that I had the presence of mind to go to my aunt's house for help.

Later that night my mother said, "What made you think of Aunt Sarah when you fell? I mean I'm so glad that you did—I don't know what else you could have done—"

"Well, of course, I thought of her. She's always been pretty good to me. I was never involved in the quarrels you had with her. Besides she has never heard me call her 'long shoes.'"

"And don't ever dare to let her hear you say that."

Nate knew that Sarah's analysis was right. (And so did I.) What a pair my parents made! He tended to do almost everything wrong, and she would quickly make him face his mistakes. So, while my mother was a warm and loving person who cared for her family, who gave everyone an ear to listen to their troubles with 110% attention, she had the analytical ability to see the major flaws in one's personality or behavior. Somehow, she thought it was her duty to let them know about it because as she said, "Who knows; maybe, they can change their ways."

And I would learn later—too late to tell Dora—that in life there are times when you may step on someone's shoes and that may be okay, but don't ruin their shine!

Nate

Would such insight have changed her? I also learned that change is the most demanding thing a person can do.

Chapter 28

About midway through college, I had an inner sense that there were many facets of my father's life and personality that were troubling and even mysterious. I decided to learn more about him through my grandmother who had an apartment in the Bronx.

"This may seem a little odd to you, Grandma, but I've come to talk to you about my father. I'm sure you know that ever since I was a little boy I have loved and admired him very much. I still do. I don't really understand him though and have come to talk to you about his childhood and how he made some of his decisions."

She moved about in her kitchen slowly, partly because of her age and partly because she suffered with chronic bronchitis. There was always a wheezing and whistling sound in her breathing.

She made herself a cup of coffee in her customary way, which was to first brew the coffee and then put it in a little pot with milk and boil it.

"I like it very hot because it opens up my lungs so I can breathe a little easier."

She sat down with her cup of coffee and took a tablet of sugar, which she broke into many small pieces, and put one on her tongue as she drank the coffee. I remembered this custom of hers since I was a small boy.

"Your father was a sort of hero in our little Jewish community outside of Newark, New Jersey. Back when he was a teenager, we went through some very disturbing times. A group of the Christian boys were attacking our synagogue at night using paint and hammers and breaking windows. Your father, who had the nickname Tootsie back then (she had a big smile when she repeated his nickname), helped to put together a group of Jewish boys who were determined to expose this anti-Semitism and put a stop to the vandalism. It seems that they made a date with those other boys to meet one night in one of the parks in our neighborhood. As I understand the story, the boys stood about 20-30 yards apart, and they started yelling anti-Semitic insults, threatening to get rid of all the Jews in the neighborhood.

"One of the gentile boys separated from the group and came closer. He was tall with a muscular build under a crop of pale blond hair. In the darkness he hid a broomstick behind his legs. Nate also separated from his friends and walked up to the blonde boy.

"'What's all this about? How about cutting this crap out? We know what you been doing, and it's got to stop,' he said.

"'What's it about? Don't make me laugh. We hate your guts, and we want you to get out of this neighborhood.'

"Nate thought something looked strange about this boy. Something was wrong with his trousers. Of course—his trouser legs were much too short—maybe two or three inches above his ankles.

"'Hey, Polack, where did you get those pants?' Nate said looking down at his feet. 'Why don't you tell your shoes to give a party and invite your pants down!'

"This infuriated the boy.

"Nate continued, 'Why do you people hate us? We haven't done anything to you. What have you got against Jews?'

"'You people killed Christ. It's right in *The Bible*. You work for the devil; you are evil Christ killers.'

Nate

"While yelling at Nate, the blonde boy swung his broomstick and with great force struck him across the legs. Nate fell to his knees in great pain. He became furious and uncontrollable with anger. He quickly stood up swinging both arms and wrists wildly. Like a prizefighter, he threw a right-handed punch in the direction of the boy's head. Nate knew a few things about boxing too.

"Right at that very moment, one of the other boys yelled, 'Woji, watch out the cops are coming.'

"The blonde boy looked away, not seeing your father's punch as it landed hard right in the middle of his face. Fearing the police, the boys turned and started to run. Nate caught a quick glimpse of that tough guy covering his bloody face.

"The reason I say that your father was a hero is because the vandalism tapered off, and the anti-Semitism was reduced to a few remarks and shouts now and then.

"I never thought of your father as a fighter, and so this incident was a surprise. Like his father he was a kind and nonaggressive-type person. But, of course, he loved prize fighting on the radio. He loved everything in sports especially baseball. He was in the playground or in the streets all the time and that's all he cared about. He was a football player on his high school team, and he was a catcher on his baseball team and he won medals at track meets. But for books and studies and homework, there was little hope.

"Finally, I was received a call from his high school principal saying that he was hopelessly behind and that I should take him out of school. We put him in a prep school hoping that individual attention from the teachers and principal would help, but that didn't work either. His father and I are partly responsible because we had two businesses to run. We had a children's clothing shop in Bloomfield and a few blocks away a dry cleaner. We spent many hours with our businesses and neglected your father.

"However, I should say that his older sister, your Aunt Ruth, at the same time was an excellent student and went ahead and got a PhD in psychology. In fact, I wonder if you knew that when Israel was granted statehood, she and her family became Israeli citizens, and she was given the responsibility of interviewing and finding jobs for all the displaced persons who survived the Holocaust and were coming to Israel, the only hope for thousands of Jews at that time.

"So your father dropped out of school and took a job, and I worried that he would never be able to support a family. He told me that he really had no interest in marriage and family. And I believed him. He cared only about sports and pretty women. My hope for him was that someday he would meet a wealthy woman who would love him for his humor; my daughters bragged that he was so handsome. Having plenty of money of her own, such a woman would not care about how much he could earn. I was disappointed in that respect when he married your mother, who had no money or profession. I pictured them living week to week and that's exactly what happened. Yes, Nate should have married a wealthy girl. He would entertain her, and she would pay the bills.

"I don't think your mother understood my hopes for your father. I think she thought that I did not like her or approve of her background. That was not the case at all. Your mother was a giving, caring person. She did so much for me when I was sick. I told her many times, 'Dora, I wish for you a long life.'"

"Grandma, you seem to be a real good business lady, but I can't see my grandfather keeping up with you and running your business."

"He was not a business person; he was a kind, good man who spent most of his time praying. In fact, he was not my choice for husband. When I was a teenager, I went to a folk dance put on by the local temple. That evening I met a young man by the name of Altman whose family had started a beautiful and successful department store in

New York City. One thing led to another and we fell in love and wanted to marry. It would have been a rich life for me, but my parents forbade the marriage because he was not an Orthodox Jew. They had picked out a man for me, a kind and religious man, a righteous man. And so, I married your grandfather. I was always the boss and the decision maker, and he took care of the religious stuff.

"He had a partner in the dry-cleaning business, as I mentioned, who was a friend of his. They both financed the purchase. He was a naïve man and did not notice that his partner was slowly cheating him out of everything.

"And so now you have a good idea of the environment that your father grew up in. Not the best, but he was loved. I would say that he was loved mostly because he made us laugh and he entertained us. He was a joy to be around."

I said, "goodbye," not knowing that it would be my last visit with her. Her eyes were wet when I left. My thoughts turned to Nate's childhood. I was determined to put all these pieces together. I wanted to understand him better. How did growing up with a weak, passive father affect him? I had hoped that a deep understanding of him would offset the disappointments that were creeping into my mind. Aside from is humor, my father was a passive man—now I discovered that his father was passive—it's my turn now—will I as the third-generation also be a passive man?

The visit with my grandmother taught me a lot about my father; however, it seemed to raise more questions. For some time I had been thinking about talking to a psychiatrist who might help me understand more about Nate and about myself and maybe even help me shape a better course for my life. I thought about it until one day, after experiencing a powerful dream, I finally made up my mind.

In my dream I stood on a lawn next to a scarecrow attached to large wooden stick that was stuck in the ground. It was an ordinary scarecrow that I had seen in books and movies with one major difference; it had my father's face. With tremendous anger, I lifted the scarecrow off the stick by its ankles and then raised it above my head and brought it crashing down shoulders and head first. Next, I repeated it with more force and then again with greater force and again with what seemed like uncontrollable anger and a desire to destroy.

Chapter 29

"In our past meetings, you've told me a lot about your life and your family. Now I'd like to hear more about how you feel today. What is troubling you now and what you would like to change?"

I had researched the best psychiatrists in New York City and decided that Dr. Abrahams would be right for me. I didn't know what to expect in this process, but I was an unhappy man determined to make some changes.

"Well, doctor, it seems that at work some of my colleagues are getting promoted ahead of me. These are people who have the same experience, same skills, and same achievements I do. In fact, in some cases their record is weaker than mine. One difference is that they are a lot more self-confident, more forceful, and sometimes even aggressive. I never thought that aggressiveness was the key to leadership and promotions.

"Tennis is the only sport that I really like, but when I play I get a terrible pounding in my head. I never seem to be able to play up to my level. I miss points and lose games far more than I should. In general, I tend to lose at any game I play. In a strange way that I can't quite explain, I seem to be more comfortable with losing them with winning.

"Another big issue for me is my marriage. I'm not sure why I married her. I have come to dislike her; it's not fair for her or me."

"You've mentioned your mother many times, and she appears in several of your dreams. Have you ever thought that there was too much mother in your childhood?"

"A number of people have mentioned that to me, of course, in a subtle way."

"Many in my profession have found that when a boy's childhood has 'too much mother,' it's often accompanied by 'not enough father.'"

"As I've mentioned my father was a lot of fun, and I really did like to be around him, but he never had any serious conversations with me. He seemed to show no interest in my problems or my future.

"But I don't seem to connect the idea of not enough father with the problems I've mentioned," I added.

"You know, when you first came into my office I saw a tall, strong man with a reasonable amount of confidence. I was totally surprised when you started to talk. Your voice is so low, so hushed. It's almost like you're afraid that you might offend someone with your words."

"I guess I still don't follow what you're getting at."

"We've known for a long time that young boys have an exaggerated idea of their strength; you can see this in their play and in certain conversations with them. Now I have had the impression that of all the things we can say about your father, we can't say that he was a strong person. In fact, it sounds like he was not particularly assertive, maybe passive. Now think of yourself as a young boy with a natural inclination to exaggerate your strength. I see in you the capacity to be a very strong person, a trait probably passed to you through your mother who was strong as was her father. Consider the fact that he had a successful taxi business in Poland and then built a big bakery here. This whole picture presents a psychological dilemma to a young boy. In other words, a young boy may fear asserting his strength to a father he perceives as weak. This dilemma is something we should investigate."

Nate

He continued, "As you grew older, you became increasingly aware of your potential strengths while at the same time you began to see his weaknesses. This presented a conflict regarding how to interact with him. One possible resolution to this conflict was for you to submerge your growing instincts to preserve the dominance of your father as head of the house. Another instinct was to destroy him as in the scarecrow dream. Of course, our society keeps those instincts in check. The best resolution is for the boy to aim to be like him and even someday marry a woman like his mother. In your case you decided, at least subconsciously, not to challenge his position in the family. It seems, based on what we know so far of your life, that you sabotaged the development of your strengths in view of the obvious weaknesses in your father."

You know the story of Oedipus who unknowingly overcame his father and married his mother. When he discovered this, he plucked out his eyes through feelings of guilt. In psychiatry we see this story in its symbolic form and, of course, not to be taken literally, but we do believe that a boy in your situation can put dampers on his own development out of fear and guilt of appearing stronger than his father. The fear is, of course, groundless. By contrast, in a healthy family situation, the young boy gets a clear picture of his father's talents and successes and decides, perhaps unconsciously, that he will someday be like him and maybe even marry a woman who's just as nice as his mother. In this case the boy will feel free to seek the full development of his manhood."

"In my situation I certainly didn't want to grow up to be like my father. In fact, I wanted just the opposite because I was afraid of failing. On the other hand, I remember feeling awkward and uncomfortable telling my father about some of the good things that were happening to me at school. I think in many ways I did force myself to continue to feel and act like a young child even though I was growing up to be a young man."

"Freud wrote an essay which in a way is an extension of the Oedipus theory, and he called it 'People Wrecked by Success.' It had been shown clinically back then that some people developed serious illness, not out of frustration, but rather from success. Without a strong father to test and retest their growing strength, some boys grow to adult men with strong feelings of guilt derived from what they have achieved or desire to achieve. Young men may develop very strong inner conflicts between the desire to achieve success on the one hand and the fear of retribution by a father with imagined anger. So, in these cases one grows up desiring success while at the same time fearing it and maybe avoiding it. Such conflicts can lead to disease."

"So, I suppose one could extrapolate from Freud's essay to say that a person can be wrecked while striving for success even before attaining it," I said.

"The truth is, based on everything we know, you are a strong and aggressive individual. The important thing to learn from all of this is that you can be just as strong as your natural abilities allow. These fears which originate in childhood are based upon fantasy and imagination; there is no punishment for being who you truly are.

"You can practice a more aggressive attitude toward me in this office. I have put up with a lot worse. I want you to try out this new approach in this office just to experience how safe and even gratifying it can be."

Later I took the subway home. It was crowded. I grabbed hold of an overhead bar, stood up straight, and took as much space as I needed. The sway of the train and the noise of the air rushing by reminded me of the many happy subway trips I took with my father. I thought back to summer times listening to baseball games with him. Smiling, I proudly pictured him bat in hand, swinging at the ball and knocking it out of the park. Then I thought, "Okay, Nate it's my turn now. I'm going to allow myself to be who I really am. I will always love him, but now he must see me as I truly am—a free man."

Chapter 30

"Then our mouths were filled with laughter...."
— *Psalm 126:2*

Dr. Klein said, "Okay, Nate, let's go over the results of your recent annual exam. Before we go into any details, I am pleased to say you are in very good health. Of course, you've got some arthritis here and there, but at your age that's expected. I am just so impressed. At the age of 95, you are in such good health and honestly you don't look anything like your age."

Nate replied, "Who would have dreamed that I would still be alive at this age? There is none of this in my family."

"There have been a lot of studies on the effects of humor on the function of the body disease and longevity and it's all positive. I mean now we know that a sense of humor is good for our health," said Dr. Klein.

"I like to joke around. Even as a kid I was not much of a student because I wanted to have fun and play, and I was crazy about sports. I hung around with a bunch of kids who liked to laugh and tell jokes and find fun wherever we could."

Interrupting Nate, Dr. Klein added, "Listen, Nate, I meet many, many people in this very room who like to joke around and have good sense of humor. But with you it's a different story. You are very special. I don't know how to say it, but humor is such a big part of you as if it's in your DNA."

"Well, it's been a pretty hard life. I couldn't hold a job for many, many years. I disappointed Dora and I haven't been a great father. I'm tired now and when I think back I don't know how I did it all. Maybe you're right; maybe joking around like I do is what got me through."

Dr. Klein said, "I've been in a study group at the synagogue in which, among other things, we are looking at the Kabbalah. This is, as I'm sure you know, the spiritual side of Judaism which reviews what wise men of old have said about the serious side of life and death and the soul." Klein shrugged his shoulders and smiled, then he raised arms slightly as if to say, "This is all new to me but who knows?" Then he resumed, "I think the soul that was given to you at birth was looking for a body that would cheer it up, so your soul was matched with a body that was destined to become this funny guy Nate, but of course what do I know about it; I'm just beginning to learn. But there is one thing I'm sure of, your sense of humor is not something superficial and maybe not worldly. I suspect rather it comes, with a purpose, from the Creator."

At this point they ended their meeting, Nate walked over to the door, looked back toward the doctor smiling and said, "I'll send you a bill, doctor, when I get home."

Chapter 31

Nate and Dora retired in Cape Cod where they rented a small subsidized apartment a couple of blocks from downtown Hyannis. The walk downtown was good exercise for Nate. He made the trip a few times a day and made good friends with many of the merchants. While he thought that Cape Cod was too cold for a decent retirement, he did appreciate the fact that there was almost no snow in the winter, which was a welcome change from Binghamton.

Dora became active in the Cape Cod Synagogue. She joined the choir and took Sunday School classes in Judaism, Bible, and Hebrew language. Her studies and a close relationship with the rabbi led to her decision to become a bat mitzvah at the age of 65, a remarkable accomplishment admired by the entire congregation.

Not content to stop there, she continued to amaze her friends by providing homemade matzo balls for the Passover Seder conducted at the synagogue. She knew that her matzo balls were better than others and became determined, despite her tiny kitchen, to make enough for the entire congregation. How she accomplished that was impressive feat. The apartment had a tiny kitchen with barely enough room for one person. She would cook a dozen or two matzo balls using every square inch of space, and then drive them to the large freezer in the synagogue. By repeating this routine several times in the months prior to the holiday, she would accumulate enough frozen matzo balls for the Seder. The congregation was by now in awe of what she could do when she set her mind to it. The Seders were well attended by the congregation who raved about the flavor and lightness of Dora's matzo balls.

There was a joke Nate loved to tell at the annual Seder. "In New York City, a beggar approached a Jewish lady with outstretched hand and said, 'Please lady, please, I haven't eaten for two weeks.' She replied shaking her finger, 'You should force yourself!'"

Nate was proud of his own contribution to the synagogue. When Nate and Dora first arrived in Cape Cod, the synagogue was situated in an old, large wood-frame house much too small for the growing population. The congregation formed a building committee with a plan to build a new modern synagogue big enough for the entire Cape Jewish population. Financing the project was a major obstacle because most of the congregants were retired, living on tight budgets.

The committee came up with the idea of renting a large hall once a week for a bingo game open to the entire Cape population, setting a price of about $.50 per game. Prizes were substantial. The committee had heard that many Christian churches were financed by bingo. Why not a synagogue? Nate answered the call for volunteers to work the bingo game. He sold the cards, arranged the seating, emptied ashtrays, and generally greeted people with a smile and maybe a few jokes.

The games were immensely successful. People came from all over. They chatted, made new friends, and showed each other how close they came to winning the previous game. While playing and talking, they smoked and smoked and smoked. The air became laden with tobacco smoke; by the end of the evening, Nate's clothing was so saturated with the smell that Dora would not let him in the house. She made him remove his clothing in the hallway and put on clean ones while she threw the tobacco-drenched stuff in the laundry.

About two years later a new and stunning synagogue stood in Hyannis with beautiful services and classes for young and old. The group of people who had formed the nucleus of the congregation and had planned and carried out the building program were proud of their determination. They had made it happen with limited resources.

Sabbath Services in the new synagogue were very well attended . People enjoyed the beautiful sanctuary and the spacious social meeting hall. Nate met the other congregants with a smile and joked around with them and sometimes got engaged in a political discussion. Dora made close friendships with the other women of the congregation most of whom were from Boston and had a noticeable Boston accent. In fact after a few years she started to pick up a Boston accent herself. Dora enjoyed these new friendships. Unfortunately and sadly, since Dora lived to the age of 99, she lost many of them on the way.

Joe Rosen was a man his 70s who they met in the Friday night social gatherings. Joe had a long white mustache which pointed downwardly on both sides, and, along with a slightly protruding mouth and chin reminded Nate of a walrus. At home they joked about him and had a few laughs, but the fun stopped when Nate observed that the walrus was paying particular attention to Dora. Increasingly week after week his interest in her was noticeably warm and friendly. It was becoming obvious that the walrus had taken a special liking to Dora. She was flattered; and, in fact, enjoyed the warm attention that she was getting. It was many years since she felt any particular romantic attachment. Her view of walrus changed. She no longer thought that the walrus joke was funny and in fact she began to defend him.

"He's a very warm and friendly man and he's just looking for somebody to talk to"

Nate found himself in a very awkward position as he saw this relationship getting closer and closer. He thought the manly thing to do was to intercede and break it up, but on the other hand he had too much pride to show that he was jealous. In fact a romantic triangle in the 70s seemed a bit ludicrous to him.

Nate's dilemma was resolved in a couple of months as the walrus became inappropriately forward. Dora and Nate agreed that it was time to have a gentle but firm conversation with the walrus.

Nate spent most of his time watching baseball and football on TV. In fact, once I saw him listening to a football game on the radio through earbuds while watching another game on TV. He made frequent walks to downtown Hyannis where, during the tourist season, there were big crowds of vacationing people and much to see and do.

Dora and Nate had all the necessities including plenty of food on the table and good medical care while living a Spartan life on Social Security checks. I believe that my mother was aware that among her siblings and my father's siblings, she and Nate retired with the lowest standard of living. As a parallel, in college I was aware that, among all the students I knew, I was by far the least financially prepared for college. There was no doubt that Nate was a poor provider. He would say that he was unlucky in business, but I think he realized that there was more than luck involved. And whatever that was, whatever the components of these failures were, I believe he deeply regretted some of the decisions in life that he had made. While he looked and acted healthy and relatively young in his 90s, I could see a hint of sadness in his eyes.

I understood that sadness as I stood next to him that day for the last time. Precious childhood memories rushed through my mind—listening to baseball games together, catching his crazy curveballs, the excitement I felt as I ran to meet him coming home. I still remember the feelings of joy and love of those days. I was a lucky kid to have him as my father.

Chapter 32

As Nate's family and friends were saying goodbye for the last time, another conversation was taking place in a faraway place. With great curiosity, the Lord spoke once more to Nate's soul, "Did you find Nate to be a funny and entertaining man?"

"For many centuries, your messengers have tried to teach that each human being should break out of his own skin and interact with other people. It was always promised that prayer for others and honorable deeds would help one to overcome physical and mental pain. In fact, one of the worst pains a mortal may suffer is to be totally lost and absorbed in one's own self.

"In Nate, I found a man who through humor could reach out to those around him leaving the confines of his own self. He saw the humorous side of life's situations and through his humor did the same for others. Through his humor, he helped others deal with their pain. In so doing, he found peace and comfort for himself.

"Nate made mistakes, exposed his ineptness, and felt shame. He was vulnerable but always had enough courage to keep trying.

"His legacy is the lesson that success and failure can be moderated with humor and a light heart, never hiding from life out of shame."

The Lord listened intently and was pleased.

CPSIA information can be obtained
at www.ICGtesting.com
Printed in the USA
FFHW02n1644040818
47632325-51204FF

9 781944 662288